THE DRUID AND THE WOLF
Prophecy of the White Wolf

By
Olivia NJ Hamel

The Druid and the Wolf Copyright © 2012 by Olivia Hamel
2016 Edition Copyright © 2016 by Olivia Hamel
Cover Art Copyright © 2016 by Olivia Hamel

All rights reserved. No part of this publication may be reproduced or transmitted in any form or by any means, whether it be electronic recording, photocopying or otherwise without written permission from Olivia Hamel.

For permissions, write to OliviaHamelBooks921@gmail.com

Hamel, Olivia.
The druid and the wolf/ Olivia Hamel
Cover art by Olivia Hamel
Prophecy of the white wolf
Summary: A druid physician has prophesied the coming of a great white wolf that will save them. Soon, a white wolf pup is found in the forest and taken into the druid clan. After being raised by the clan for a year, the king of a nearby city decides to capture the druids and attempt to have them executed. After setting off on a journey to learn how to fight, will she make it back in time to save her beloved family?

ISBN-13: 978-1535094139

ISBN-10: 1535094133

Dedicated to my grandfather Edward B. Kevins.

CHARACTERS

SASCHA: A young white she-wolf with green eyes.

AKEMI: Gray she-wolf with lighter underfur and darker gray speckles and blue eyes.

AVYRUS: A tall black haired young man with icy blue eyes. He is the King of the druid clan.

TAIREK: A brown haired man with yellow-green eyes. He is the physician to the druid clan.

TITUS: Tan skinned druid warrior with black hair and amber eyes.

ZACHERY: Young man with brown hair and green eyes. He is the physician apprentice of the druid clan.

KING XANTHUS DE TASKE: Black wavy hair with brown eyes. He is the King of Aerulis.

QUEEN ANNE DE TASKE: Ginger colored hair with green eyes. She is the queen of Aerulis.

SIR WILLIAM: A knight of Aerulis.

SIR CADOC: A knight of Aerulis.

MILLIE: A young serving girl from Aerulis with beautiful, long, slightly curly light brown hair and the brightest blue eyes.

THOR: Gigantic brown male wolf with pale underfur, three darker brown stripes on his back, and blue eyes.

TALOMI: A white male wolf with ice blue stripes and amber eyes.

ORION: White male wolf with orange stripes and amber eyes.

STRAWBERRY: Black she-wolf with red swirly markings.

RIZA: She-wolf with ginger fur and lighter underfur.

HARLOC: A powerful dragon that lives in the Meadows of Agrona.

REI: Gray eyes, no hair, tan skin, and many scars. Even scars on his scalp.

KING DRAGOMIR: Gray hair with a large bald spot on the entire top of his head. Also, he has blue-gray eyes. He is the King of Windstorm City.

CHINO: A male Neapolitan mastiff that helps Sascha in the war against Harloc.

OKINA: A gray she-wolf with green stripes and red eyes. Member of the Twilight Pack.

ADAM: A male Irish wolfhound that helps Sascha in the war against Harloc.

KURO: Jet-black male dragon. He is a warrior of Doragontaigun.

SKY WING: Ice blue dragoness with purple eyes. She is a warrior of Doragontaigun.

JASMINE: Golden colored dragoness. She is a warrior of Doragontaigun.

STONE: Gray wolf with blue eyes.

HIKARU: Golden furred she-wolf with green eyes.

IZOR: Jet black male wolf with blue eyes.

SNOWDROP: White and gray she-wolf with yellow eyes.

TSUTE: Dark brown wolf with blue eyes.

SIBER: Stone gray wolf with orange eyes.

THUNDERMIST: White she-wolf with sorrel colored patches and blue eyes.

SORREL: Sorrel colored she wolf with green eyes.

EVIA: Gray she-wolf with dark green eyes.

SHIN: Black wolf with white underfur and purple eyes.

JASON: Orange wolf with blue eyes.

TASGALL: Light brown wolf with yellow eyes.

AMARA: Yellow she-wolf with dark blue eyes.

ZURI: Orange she-wolf with white underfur and brown eyes.

AERON: Black wolf with green eyes.

YORATH: Cream colored wolf with yellow eyes.

KIRA: Cream colored wolf with magenta patches and blue eyes.

PROLOGUE

The moon was covered by dark storm clouds, rain stinging the man's scarred arms like needles. The pine treetops looked like black figures above him, revealing the mottled blue-gray sky. Squeezing the rain water out of his brown hair, he walked to the door of the King's Shed. It was the biggest of all the sheds in the druid camp. "Avyrus, I must speak with you immediately!" the druid physician called out, knocking his rough hands on the door. Thunder crashed above like a great tree colliding with the ground in a fall. "It cannot wait," he added impatiently. To Tairek the druid King seemed to be taking a long time, but it was probably just his anxiety. The visions he had seen in his nightmare were repeating in his mind now. That was why Tairek was so determined to address King Avyrus about the matter.

Oh, how the glowing green orbs of the being's eyes and the huge blood stained fangs were haunting him right now. Where was Avyrus? He was about to knock again before the druid King opened the door with surprise and a tad bit annoyance in his blue glare. The druid physician could sense how Avyrus was trying to hide his annoyance. Tairek did not blame him for being annoyed, though. Being awoken after a very stressful day wasn't exactly pleasurable. The King sighed, letting go of his irritation. "What could it possibly be now? I only hope it is important," he told his physician. Avyrus gestured for Tairek to come in, walking back into the shed. Tairek nodded in respect for his King and walked into the dryness and welcoming warmth of the King's Shed. Avyrus turned to face him, his blue eyes glaring at him expectantly. "Well, what have you to tell me that is so vital?" He asked, nodding for the druid physician to explain the matter.

Tairek hung his head for a moment; he didn't know where to begin. There was so much to tell! Raising his glare to the druid King, he spoke in a deep voice, "I have received visions of things to come."

Instantly, Avyrus' calm expression turned into a more serious look. He understood now that this was very important. "Please, go on," the King urged.

Tairek let a few seconds of silence pass, and then described what he had seen. "I foresee the coming of a great white wolf with eyes the color of the green grass. She will be forced on a journey to save us."

King Avyrus was speechless. His icy blue eyes shone with something similar to fear, but the druid King shook it away quickly. "A wolf?" he began, raising an eyebrow in confusion. "But how can a wolf save us? It is an animal."

"I don't know," Tairek hung his head, feeling slightly ashamed that he had no answer for his King. "We will have to wait and see for ourselves. It is all we can do right now."

Avyrus gave a long and stressful sigh and walked slowly to the mouth of the shed. He gazed up at the stormy sky, thinking carefully. "You have always been good at predicting the future, Tairek. I trust what you are saying," the King spoke in a very calm voice, still glaring up at the storm clouds as the rain collided loudly onto the ground. A streak of lightning lit up the entire sky for just a split second. "If what you are saying is true," Avyrus said quietly but was still heard over the crackling of the rain, "then the wolf will save us."

Four sunrises later everything was very quiet. Avyrus went about his duties as King of the druid clan. He had sent out patrols to check the territory for any signs of invasion. He had also sent out hunting patrols to retrieve food for the clan. It seemed like a normal, peaceful day in Rosewood Forest. The sun offered its welcoming warmth, and the air was as sweet as flowers themselves.

"My lord," A druid rushed up to the King, whom was sitting upon a large boulder. The man had been with two others whom had parted with him moments earlier, and Avyrus looked up to see who they were. Yes, the hunting patrol he had sent out earlier had at last returned. But he did not see any prey with his men. Now how strange was that? They had never failed to return with food, and even if there had been a prey shortage they would have hunted for days if they had to. There was just something about this that he couldn't place his finger on.

"Yes, Titus?" Avyrus dipped his head for the druid warrior to explain. What could possibly be the explanation for this? It had better be good. "Why have you brought no food? There had better be good reason for this." Titus was a dark skinned man with clothing of the common folk. He had bright amber eyes, which apparently attracted women constantly. Avyrus could not understand why they liked his personality though, for Titus was far too arrogant to raise a family. But then again, that was none of the King's business.

"There is!" Titus began, slightly out of breath. "I do not know what significance it is to you, but we have found a wolf pup. It is a few days old."

Avyrus gave a light gasp; a wolf pup? How coincidental was that? Tairek had prophesied the coming of a white wolf, and out of nowhere his warriors find a lone wolf pup in the forest? The King needn't fake the shock on his face.

Avyrus knew that it would be difficult, perhaps impossible; to nourish the pup with milk that was not from a mother wolf... but it was worth a try. A wolf pup that age would most definitely not survive without its mother to nurse it. But the wolf pup had to live! It sounded mad, but that wolf held the future of the entire druid clan in its paws. It had to survive, or else. "There must be a way," he muttered to himself, and then gave his warrior a stern look. "Take me to this wolf pup, immediately."

The young druid warrior took him to the pup, inside the Medicine Shed. King Avyrus squatted beside the pup, which was lying on the warm blankets, shrieking with hunger. The small puppy was fully engulfed in snow white fur, and when Avyrus stroked it's back it felt as if he were stroking silk. The wolf pup reached for his hand and weakly bit into his index finger, a frustrated growl rumbling from its throat. It did not hurt him, for it was only a starved young puppy. Pulling his hand away the wolf pup held its grip on his finger and gave a light tug. The wolf pup let out a squeak and began to suckle on the King's finger. Avyrus raised both eye brows and smiled down at the wolf. In fact, he found it quite adorable as he did any young animal that seemed to like him. He searched the pup's eyes to identify the color, and when he saw them his heart sunk. This wolf was the one Tairek had prophesied! She had arrived to them! The pup's grass green eyes seemed to glow and stare right through his soul. "Bring Tairek to me at once," he ordered Titus sternly. "Tell him that the wolf has arrived."

"What do you mean, my lord?" Titus queried.

"Go!"

Titus nodded curtly and was off to notify the druid physician of the wolf pup. A few minutes later, Tairek rushed into the shed and squatted on the opposite side of the wolf pup. "This is the wolf I saw in my dreams, sire," Tairek said with confidence. "I never forget a face. This is the only wolf I've ever seen with green eyes, because usually wolves have golden eyes."

Avyrus played around with his finger, tugging it lightly back and forth. The wolf pup clung onto his index finger with its small fangs, continuing to 'suckle'. The King let out a light sigh, "She has to live, but she is too young to survive without her mother," and said with a worriedly voice. "There's nothing we can do."

"Don't talk like that!" Tairek growled. He was daring to growl at his King, but only because they had been close friends since childhood. It was rare he made that approach though, for he knew it would become abused if he did it frequently. But now was a very good exception for it. "I know that one of the hunting dogs will not nurse her and that she is too young to digest meat. However, I once knew this woman who found an abandoned dog pup and raised it on goat's milk. I do not know if it will work with a wolf, but we must do everything within our power to ensure her survival."

"Alright," King Avyrus nodded, a surge of relief rushing through him. "We have plenty of goats. Now all we need is someone willing to raise a wolf."

Tairek smiled at the King, "I can get my apprentice to raise her. Since the wolf is so young he will have to feed her drops off his fingers, which will be time consuming but worth it."

"Then it is settled," Avyrus dipped his head gratefully. "But what shall we name her?"

"Well... every time I think of the dream I had of the wolf, I keep thinking of the name Sascha," Tairek said. "Perhaps it is a sign that this must be her name?"

"Then Sascha will be her name," Avyrus agreed.

CHAPTER ONE

Sascha spent the night inside the Medicine Shed at the foot of Zachery's bed. The physician apprentice had been the one to raise her and instinctively she felt a bond with him. If she went back through her memories, Zachery had been quite disappointed with having to raise her. He had complained and growled, and had been impatient about having to feed her every three hours for a couple months. It had been a bit easier for him once she had adjusted to meat at two months old.

The white she-wolf tossed and turned that night; she could hardly sleep at all! When she did happen to get a few moments of sleep she always ended up waking up with a terrifying jolt. After a while she just climbed up onto Zachery's mattress weightlessly and practically collapsed onto her side with exhaust. The druid physician's close body was keeping her warm, while she also kept him warm with her own body heat... which was an essential thing for the season of late fall! Actually Sascha really had no problem with the cold it brought, except that it meant lesser food. That was what made it uncomfortable. A wolf with an empty stomach wasn't the best thing to have in the camp.

But that didn't mean that the clan had to starve because of her. Because she was an animal her clan had to eat first, and unfortunately the food supply had been so low lately that she had only been able to nibble on a few scraps of meat. But she was willing to make the sacrifice for her clan's sake. Still, at least it had not snowed yet.

Again she woke up with a jolt. Zachery was so cold to the touch, which made Sascha want to warm him. She put her muzzle on his shoulder to hopefully make him feel better. She couldn't tell whether he was awake or asleep, but she kind of figured he was wakeful. What human could possibly sleep in this weather? She couldn't figure out what was keeping her up. Whenever she dozed off beside the fire pit she dreamed of only peaceful things. Like hunting with Zachery, frolicking in the prairies outside Rosewood Forest, and all the things a wolf would love to do.

Sascha fell asleep for just a moment. She saw nothing but pitch blackness. Suddenly a choking smell hit her throat. It was so vivid! She could have sworn that it was real and that's why she was so scared. She had scented something similar to this near the fire pit. Sascha was awakened from her short slumber by Zachery's stirring beside her, and she lifted her head from his shoulder. It must have been the cold that was irritating him. But then a split second later, Zachery sat up and threw his blankets off. He grabbed his robe to cover up his nakedness and ran out of the Medicine Shed. "Zachery?" She barked, a feeling of dread sparking in her heart. Sascha knew he'd never understand her and that her words sounded like wolfish barks and howls to him, but she didn't care. She often did this, just to communicate with him.

Instantly she shot up and bounded out of the shed after Zachery. That was when she noticed the same choking smell from her dream existed in the waking world. When she lay her eyes upon what surrounded the druid camp, her eyes went wide with terror. Fire was engulfing the entire forest!

Her nightmare had become a reality! "Fire in the camp...!" Zachery screamed as he ran through the camp, and then started to break out in a fit of coughing as the black smoke hit him. "We must evacuate!"

Sascha had to do something. Anything! These were her people and she'd been raised with them. They were her family! Sascha started running wildly around the camp letting out loud howls of terror, hoping that it would get the druids out faster. Within seconds the camp was swarming with humans, yelling with fear. Sascha looked to the camp's entrance and saw the flames that were about to block the exit. Quickly, she searched the druids for Zachery but no matter how hard she searched she could not see his agile body. Usually she'd recognize him by the way his brown hair was styled, but he was nowhere to be seen. It was as if the smoke of the fire had devoured him within seconds, and Sascha knew that she had never felt so scared and alone than in this one moment. Time seemed to slow down, and everything felt like a painful eternity. The heat of the fire stung her face as she approached it, and the sulfur was coloring her pelt dark grey.

Sascha dashed toward the exit of the druid camp as fast as her paws would carry her, starting to pant heavily from the strain and suddenly breaking out in a fit of coughing from the blasted smoke that was beginning to fill her lungs. Before she could reach the exit the hand of a human reached out and grabbed her tightly on her leather collar. She must have been so focused that she didn't see him or her. The leather collar pressured her wind pipe for a moment, thus making it impossible to breathe at all for that short period of time and also causing pain to her neck and throat. It wasn't new to her, though. For whenever she hunted with Zachery or any of the druids for that matter, they would stop her like this to keep her from running at the target. The only thing different about this was the intensity of the pain. Sascha had been running very fast, so obviously it would cause great discomfort at the least.

The man pulled her backward and forcefully led her to the other side of the camp. She quickly realized by the old man's faint grassy scent that it was the druid physician Tairek. Sascha respected him, and trusted him with her own life, but she couldn't help but wonder what was on the physician's mind. They were running in the opposite direction of the exit, and Sascha knew of no other way to escape the flames. She glanced at the opening where the rest of the clan had escaped through, and her grass green eyes widened with terror. The only possible escape had been fully engulfed in fire!

When they reached the other side of the camp, Tairek didn't stop. He just pulled her through the thorn bushes, painfully trying to ignore the sting of them breaking through his skin. Sascha was more protected because of her pelt, but that didn't mean she was fully protected. The unforgiving thorns scratched at her face, legs, arms, and stomach; thus, the wolf began to bleed. After Tairek and Sascha passed through the thorn bushes, they arrived in a clearing. She had never known that there was an emergency exit, and it didn't seem that anyone else knew either. Then again they probably did; they just didn't want their skin ripped apart by the thorns and so instead went out the main entrance. It was hard for Sascha to see, for the choking smoke was blinding her. But Tairek led her through the clearing, as quick as he could without stumbling into anything... or off anything. There was plenty of smoke, of course; but there did not seem to be much fire in this area, which was good.

Suddenly, Tairek stopped in his tracks. It took Sascha a moment to take in the scene and realize what had caused him to do so. If Tairek hadn't been looking hard enough, then they both would have plunged down off a small cliff. Despite the smoke, Sascha could see the bottom quite clearly and it didn't look like anyone would live if they were to accidentally fall off the edge. The cold, sharp rocks below were like knives sticking up out of the water while a river crashed into them endlessly.

"Stay right where you are," an authoritative English man's voice sounded behind them like a crash of thunder. Tairek and Sascha froze when these words were spoken. They heard multiple horses whinnying behind them, which Tairek knew was not a good thing. They surrounded them against the edge of the river, ensuring there was no escape. "Drop any weapons and turn around slowly," the gruff sounding man ordered harshly. Sascha looked around and noted that the other men had crossbows pointed straight at Tairek, to ensure he did not try anything. Tairek somehow knew that if he tried anything he would be shot without hesitation so he did what the group's leader said and turned around slowly, putting both of his hands up in the air and letting go of Sascha's collar. The white female wolf turned around to see the men, their angry and somewhat emotionless expressions glaring darkly at her friend. "Tairek, w-what's happening?" She whined with fear.

"Shut your dog up!" The gruff sounding man yelled.

Tairek sighed lightly, not daring to move a muscle. "Easy there, Sascha. Easy," he whispered softly, so that no one but Sascha could hear. She understood him, and lowered her head with the continuing fear of the men holding the crossbows. *Oh please,* she prayed, *please let everything be alright!*

It was hard to see the men and horses through the thick smoke, but she could make out their figures and everything she needed to know really. It was getting so hard to breathe! She could just see the orange waves of fire off in the distance. The wind was drifting the fire toward them.

"Kill the druid immediately," the leader ordered abruptly. The knights obeyed and pointed their crossbows at Tairek. Without thinking of the consequences, Sascha jumped in front of the druid physician protectively. Even though she was not raised to know the ways of the wolf and knew little about them aside from their beastly behavior, she instinctively bared her large fangs at the knights with a deeply increasing rage. Sascha felt as if she would kill them if they advanced any further toward her and Tairek. Right now, she only knew two things. One, she needed to protect Tairek. Two, she had to be brave to get through this. And those were the only two natural instincts that she would even listen to.

Sir Cadoc cursed and his horse jumped away when he saw her white fangs reveal themselves from behind her lips. The other horses did the same, spooked by the wolf. The knights had to gain control of the animals before dealing with the situation at hand. Sascha snarled, but it came out pitifully. It just wasn't the proper wolf growl. Wolf growls sounded somewhat similar to a hiss, but Sascha's sounded like a small dog's growl. But that did not mean she would stop. Only the urge to protect Tairek at all costs was driving her. She was not even thinking about how embarrassing it really was.

"Do not think I will spare a druid! You're whole clan has been rounded up and will one by one receive a traditional execution," the leader of the group spat furiously. "And so will you."

Sascha didn't wipe the ferocious look off her face, but instead looked up at the Captain Knight with slightly fearful eyes. When she really thought about it, how was she expected to protect Tairek against six armored men? It was unheard of and impossible... at least for a wolf. "Kill the half-breed," the leader ordered angrily. "It's of no use to us if it's part wolf." Sascha gasped and shot behind Tairek like a coward. They were closing in on Tairek and Sascha. Everything seemed hopeless; until the druid physician spoke up, which slowed the knights.

"Is that really what you think of me? Only a mere druid," Tairek began coldly, and then added with anger, "What happened to brother, Will? Just because I chose not to join your team of knights does not mean you can just deny that we are siblings... both sharing the same parents. You used to be a druid!"

Well, that was shameful. Sascha could not believe that Tairek had such a hateful brother. If Sascha had a brother who hated her and denied their blood relationship, and even supported her execution, then that surely would hurt. She could imagine how much it hurt Tairek, despite how much he was hiding it behind his voice. Sascha flattened her ears coldly when Sir Will replied. "I have no idea what you are talking about, fiend. The druids are a threat to my people, especially now that they are recruiting wolves to torment the villagers," the knight shot Sascha a very hateful look, but then looked back up at his brother with a territorial look in his eyes. "All druids must be rounded up, and you're the only one who hasn't run into our little trap. Good job, I must say. But you still got caught."

Sascha bared her teeth, making not even the slightest sound. She was truly a coward, but also wanted to keep Tairek safe. "Shoot them!" Will ordered his knights. Sascha knew she had less than two seconds to react.

Tairek jumped in front of the wolf, shielding her with his body. "No!" Sascha howled, but it was too late. Before she could even process it in her mind, the crossbows had shot at her friend. "No, Tairek!" She called. Only two arrows had hit him, and the other four had hit the ground. One arrow was protruding from the center of his chest and the other in his upper shoulder. The druid physician moaned with pain as he struggled to stand. "I knew my time would come soon," he smiled. "But I would never shame myself to die at the hands of you or your King." Tairek chuckled, and leaned toward the edge of the cliff. It wasn't a long way down, but it was far enough. "If I must die, I want to die to save the one that will save the druids."

What did he mean when he said 'the one that would save the druids'? Who was that? The only one Tairek had saved was Sascha. But surely she could not be the one! There was nothing significant about her; at least not in that sense! How could she save the druids?

To Sascha's horror Tairek started to edge toward the cliff, eventually stepping off. "Tairek…?" Sascha whimpered. But then she realized what he was doing. He was doing this all for her! She peeked over the edge and only caught him being dragged under the water by the current. Sascha didn't know what else to do! She had lost him! What was she to do now? Will had stated that the rest of the druids had been arrested, so where would she go now? What could she do about it? With the druid physician gone, she was in despair.

"Leave him, he'll die off eventually," Will said, and then added, "Kill the wolf, now!"

Sascha gasped with fear and whipped around when she heard those words. They instantly shot at her, but she leapt swiftly out of the way. Jumping toward the horses made them rear, and a sole knight was thrown to the ground after being caught off guard by Sascha's sudden movements. The white wolf ran down a nearby slope to the riverbank. Soon she hit the freezing water and at the same time saw Tairek struggling to stay above the surface far up ahead. Sascha risked her life swimming toward him in a loving attempt of rescue. But he had been shot through the chest; there was nothing she could do once, and if, she reached him! Then she remembered Zachery, the physician's son and apprentice. He would know what to do, but he had been arrested by the King of Aerulis. She had to try her best. It may not be expected of her, but she felt that it was required of her.

She was only a few feet away from the struggling Tairek before she saw a drop up ahead, and instantly knew what it was. Oh, why did there have to be a waterfall? Trying to speed up her pace, she finally came within inches of the druid physician. Sascha bit onto his shoulder, and bravely tried to drag him sideways to the narrow rocky shore. She even outstretched her sharp wolf claws, swimming with all her strength to reach the river bank. But in seconds the earth fell out from under her. She and Tairek dropped down the waterfall and were consumed in the deep, black, confusing water below.

Her lungs burned as she became disoriented for about ten seconds. She frantically swam up to the surface. Sascha gasped desperately for oxygen when she hit the air and climbed onto a rock by the shore, trying to catch her breath. Her eyes were half open, blurred by the stinging ice cold water that clung to her pelt and dripped into her grass green eyes. Remembering Tairek she lifted her head and opened her eyes wide, searching everywhere for him. Sascha spotted him holding weakly onto rocks nearby the bank of the river. Sascha struggled on shaky legs to a standing position, and then made her way up another rock that was attached to the bank. Once there, she dashed over to the rocks that were holding the druid physician. She made her way carefully across them, and then bit into Tairek's tan shirt to drag his half unconscious body to the shore where they would be safe from harm.

Tairek lay on the shore motionless. Her muzzle was now covered in Tairek's scarlet red blood, but she tried not to think about it. A few moments later water came gushing out of the physician's mouth and nose. The water had gotten into his lungs, but Sascha was too inexperienced to know that was fatal. The druid physician moaned with extreme pain, and looked at the white wolf with watery eyes. "Sascha..." He whispered shakily, his voice gurgling with water. She lay at his side, licking his face worriedly. "You're going to be okay, Tairek. I promise!" She barked. "I'll take care of you."

Tairek closed his eyes and sighed. "When my... father... died, he told... me... that he could... understand the language... of his dog that was whimpering beside him," he struggled to speak.

"Don't try to talk!" She growled, flattening her white ears.

"I... never believed him," the physician ignored her, his eyes opening a little bit. "But it... is so. I can finally... understand you, my dear wolf. And I must have a word... with you before... my passing over into the... afterlife."

"You're not going to die!" The white wolf exclaimed.

"Do not... be afraid, young wolf," Tairek gave her a faint smile, starting to unhook her collar. "My spirit will... live on in you. I will guide you... to your destiny."

She pulled away in surprise. "What are you talking about?" She didn't want to lose her collar either!

"Sascha, my dear wolf, I once told King Avyrus... of my nightmares about a white wolf," he said and paused. Then continued, "None of the other druids know this, but... you are the great white wolf," Tairek whispered, his chest seeming to clear moderately. Sascha knew it was very painful for him, though. More painful than she could possibly imagine, she was sure of that.

Was Tairek just delusional because he was in the process of dying? "You know that's not true, Tairek, please don't tell me that."

"Do not complicate things," Tairek said sternly. "You are the great white wolf with... the eyes the color of grass that will save us all!"

Sascha flinched when he raised his voice. She did not want him to be serious, but she knew in the back of her head that he was. She sighed and gave a curt nod to the physician, "Please, tell me more. I must know."

"We never receive straight answers, so I cannot tell you much," Tairek answered. "But... what I can tell you is that you will... have to save the druids from King Xanthus, even at the cost... of your life." The druid physician pulled something from his pocket and placed it at Sascha's front paws. It was a tiny bag filled with what the wolf believed to be coins of some sort. "This bag contains five gold coins. You will need it."

"For what, may I ask?"

"You must go and see the... the Fighting Master Rei in Windstorm City. He can speak to animals, and if you... show him this he would be more than... willing to train you." Tairek said, his voice becoming quieter. "You must go..."

Suddenly, the white wolf heard shouting and the sound of hooves off in the distance and then Tairek gave a painful shout. "Run now! I'll be alright!" He reached out and then ripped the she-wolf's collar off right over her head. And Sascha had to accept that her collar was gone, as was her last connection with the druid clan because she was going away for a while.

Sascha wanted nothing more but to stay with the druid. He had done so much for her. He had saved her life as a pup, given her a warm home in the druid clan, and convinced King Avyrus to assign her as one of the hunting dogs, among many other things. How could she just leave him here to die? "I will not betray you!" She growled sternly and then grabbed him by the shoulder with her teeth.

"The King has to be stopped!" Tairek snapped, but when Sascha did not listen he pushed her away with the last of his physical strength. "Get out..." he paused in a fit of coughing, more water rushing out of his mouth along with a few droplets of blood. It was then that he fell into unconsciousness. Or did he...?

"Tairek, please, don't leave!" She shouted, tears splashing down onto the ground. This was it. She had to be strong. She had to get through this. She had to fulfill her destiny. Tairek's life would have been wasted if she continued on being a cowardly fool. After inhaling Tairek's still warm herbal scent one last time, the white wolf picked up the bag of gold and backed away from him. She placed it down at her paws to pay her final respects to the man that she owed her life to. "May you rest in peace, old friend," she said as more tears streamed down her face, her voice beginning to crack. Sascha then picked up her bag of gold. This would never be easy, so she just braced herself and took one last look at the burning forest above.

Sascha ran down the river, forcing her legs to work at a very rapid speed. She needed to hurry to Windstorm City and have the Fighting Master teach her these skills that Tairek had mentioned in order to save her clan. There was only one problem... she did not know how to get there.

CHAPTER TWO

Sascha had run for two days. She was so tired that she could have fallen asleep as she ran. At best, she was making good ground. At worst, she had no clue where she was going. It seemed like it was utterly hopeless now. And when she walked tiresomely to the very edge of a huge steep hill, her mouth fell open at the sight that the hill overlooked. Mountains; nothing but mountains as far as the eye could see and fading off into the horizon. There was also a small streak of what she liked to call the Big Pond. It was another word for the ocean. She had... traveled across England? That was over one hundred miles! And if she did not find Windstorm City anytime soon, how was she expected to travel so far?! Especially not knowing what direction she needed to go. Sascha was stuck in the middle of nowhere, with no choice but to struggle forward. And so she did just that; made her way down the hill and continued on her blind journey with the bag of gold coins held firmly in her mouth.

The white wolf continued to walk until twilight came upon the world around her. She had never been out this late, except for the past two days. She was still very scared of the shadows the trees cast, and the illusions that the time of twilight created inside of a dark misty forest. There were no leaves on the trees because it was winter, and even though the ground and foliage was covered with white frost there was no snow in sight. The worst part of this journey so far was that she was so cold and disoriented! This winter temperature chilled her to the bone, even with her thick white coat.

When Sascha heard the breaking of dried leaves close by, anyone would imagine that it startled her greatly. What was it? Was someone watching her? Or was it just a prey animal? No, it couldn't be. Prey was extremely scarce in winter, there would not be a random animal running around. Besides, the crunching of the leaves was too heavy and not light like a mouse or a squirrel walking. Eventually the breaking branches crackled in a rhythm like footsteps and it became louder and louder, until she felt as if the being were right behind her. Spinning around trying to locate where the sounds were coming from in the dark forest, Sascha began to panic. Who was playing around with her mind? Was it a hunter? She honestly hoped not, because she really didn't have the skills to escape in time, blinded by the darkness of twilight. While in her state of terror, she saw things she never would have had she been calm; the trees started to look like skeletons and the bare bushes looked like evil creatures.

"Hello there. Are you alright?" A very soft and feminine voice spoke behind her. Sascha whipped around with her fangs bared only to see a ragged gray she-wolf giving her a friendly smile. She sensed no threat from the female, so she let her fangs disappear behind her lips for the moment. Instead, she just let out a corny growl to let the female before her know that she would not tolerate trouble.

The she-wolf chuckled innocently. "Did your pack not teach you how to snarl properly?" She inquired, tilting her head.

"My growl is perfectly fine!" Sascha snapped irritably. "Now tell me. What is your name? And what do you want with me?" Eying the she-wolf suspiciously Sascha placed down the bag of gold coins and hit it behind her white front paws.

The light gray she-wolf tilted her head and rotated her ears curiously, and then let out a huge grin. "My name is Akemi," she answered excitedly, wagging her tail to and fro. "What's yours?" This female was a gray she-wolf with lighter underfur and darker gray speckles and blue eyes. Now that Sascha thought about it Akemi did look quite unique in fur pattern. That was when the white she-wolf caught a glimpse of Akemi's bright blue eyes. They seemed to glow and shine through the darkness of the forest.

"I'm... my name is Sascha," she said blankly.

"It's a pleasure to meet you, Sascha!"

Sascha sighed, letting her muscles relax a bit. Well, it didn't look like Akemi was a threat. In fact, she didn't sound very wise either. More like a newborn pup. "Well, Akemi," she began as she sat down on the cold brown leaves. "What's your business here?"

Akemi looked down at the ground for a moment. "Actually, I'm nothing but a mere nomad," she started. "My pack cast me out, as I was a troublesome omega. I've been on my own for a long time."

What was an omega? Maybe it was one of the pack positions? Or perhaps it was another word for traitor? She had no knowledge of wolf packs, only of the druid clans. "What is an omega, may I ask?" Sascha asked in a much friendlier voice.

"It is the lowest of pack positions. Only a wolf that betrays their pack in some way receives that position," Akemi gave the explanation carefully. "They used me as bait during battles to distract our enemies. That's exactly where I got this scar from," she pointed her nose to a claw mark on her shoulder. Clumps of fur were missing on the front of her body, which Sascha assumed were from these experiences. Her story made her grateful that her mother had abandoned her as a pup for being half dog, and that King Avyrus' warriors had been miraculously able to find her and raise her in the druid clan. "One day I just refused to do as they said and the alpha cast me into exile. And that's pretty much how I ended up as a wanderer," Akemi finished, blinking multiple times and looking to side as if she were nervous talking about it. "I shouldn't be here really, and neither should you. The Twilight Forest is the Twilight Pack's territory."

The Twilight Forest, huh? She had heard of it when she was a pup. One of the hunting dogs had told her that at twilight mythical creatures would roam around and kill anything in their way. Were these legends true? Would there be magical creatures out in the wilderness, hunting her down?

"You mean... the Twilight Forest from the legends?" Sascha inquired.

"I think so," Akemi responded undecidedly. "I overheard a human say that no one has ever dared enter the Forest at night, except for the knights." She paused, thinking, then went on with a raised brow. "I would imagine that this is the Forest they're referring to."

Sascha wanted to say something in return, but Akemi started to speak before she could even open her mouth.

"Are you from around here?" She queried.

Sascha sighed when she was reminded of the druids, and shifted her white tail on the dead and dried leaves, looking away from Akemi's blue stare. "No," she replied without hesitation. "I'm from one of the druid clans."

"You mean those magic folk?" Akemi looked surprised. "Did they kidnap you from your pack?"

Sascha looked back at the lone she-wolf. "I never had a pack," she answered and then went on with a smile. "I guess you can say they just took me in before I even opened my eyes." She was beginning to like Akemi, but then again there was still that barrier; what was Akemi's opinion of magic? Maybe she was not fond of it, or the druids, for her first guess had been that they had kidnapped Sascha.

Akemi just nodded: "So why are you so far away from your clan's territory?"

"It's a long story..."

"I'm listening," she smiled brightly, eager to hear the white wolf's story. Sascha told all that had happened to her in the past few days to this hyper light gray she-wolf. Akemi was silent the entire time.

When Sascha had finished, Akemi spoke up softly as she stood up on all fours. "So you need to know where Windstorm City is so you can find this Rei person."

"Yes!" Sascha wagged her tail as she stood up as well, her bright green eyes flashing with hopefulness. "If you know, then please tell me. You'd be a friend for life if you did..."

Akemi gave a high pitched laugh at Sascha. "Is that so?" She began. "I could certainly help you. In fact, I could take you there myself."

"You would do that?"

"Of course I'd do that," Akemi winked at her and then gave a chuckle. "Well hey, when you've been kicked out of your pack and have nowhere else to be why shouldn't you try to help your fellow wolves, right?" The light gray she-wolf paused, and then added more seriously. "To your surprise I'm sure, you were heading the right way. Windstorm City's lower village is just across this forest."

This just shocked her. All Sascha had to do was travel through the Twilight Forest and then she'd instantly be at the entrance of Windstorm City's lower village, which would then lead her to the upper village? She wished that she could have figured that out by herself. "So when do you want to leave?" she asked.

"Tomorrow at dawn," Akemi answered with a nod. "You look travel worn, so you'll need rest if this Battle Master is to train you."

"No, no, I'm doing okay," Sascha protested softly.

"Nonsense," Akemi smiled and walked away from Sascha, half expecting her to follow. "I know a place not too far from here. I slept there last night."

With a quiet sigh, Sascha finally agreed and followed Akemi, picking up her well hidden bag of gold coins.

Sascha had a general idea of what was happening back at the main city of Aerulis. Due to her lack of knowledge she just assumed that the druids were sitting in a moldy dungeon, basically just waiting for her to rescue them all. But that was only half of what was really happening. King Xanthus had ordered the trial of every druid be individual, to 'make it last longer'. And the King was not feeling very merciful that morning.

Xanthus was broad in the arms and muscular in other places. He had long and wavy black hair with brown eyes. He was overweight in the stomach area, and was almost too lazy to start the trial for the druids that day. The general idea of a lazy monarch that anyone could imagine, but he enjoyed his life... not having to worry about anything, aside from his overloading duties as King of Aerulis. He had very pale skin and wavy jet-black hair. He wore casual clothes; nothing like a King should wear. He mostly wore typical commoners clothing to keep from getting too hot.

Titus, the druid warrior that had first discovered Sascha abandoned in the forest, was thrown on his knees on the throne of King Xanthus and his loyal Queen Anne. Titus let out a grunt of pain and the knights in the room laughed heartily at his misfortune. The support of his knights made Xanthus crack a smirk.

"I come before you all today to pass judgment," the King began loudly so that all could hear him well. The knights and ladies of the court listened intently, extremely curious to hear their King pass the druid's sentence. "This druid whom goes under the name Titus has broken our greatest law. He is a user of sorcery and a danger to our city." King Xanthus then looked down at the restrained druid with a look of deathly seriousness on his face. "You practice magic. Do you deny this?"

Titus hung his head, the guards holding a tighter grasp on his shoulders. "No, your majesty," he responded.

"Do you deny planning an attack against your King with wild beasts?"

"You," Titus began, "are not my King."

The King struggled to hold his hot temper with the druid warrior. Taking a deep breath to calm his nerves, he continued to press the man, pacing in front of him, "Was it not you who recruited a wolf to torment and possibly kill the villagers of Aerulis?"

Titus looked up with surprise and stammered the fearful reply: "I never did such a thing! We only took the wolf pup in to help us catch food more easily!"

Xanthus began to mock the man: "And you expect me to believe the word of a druid? Besides, I own Rosewood Forest. My father may have been a fool letting the druids lives there in peace, but I will not do the same. I am not a fool."

Titus looked down at his knees again, his heart racing and stomach aching with a sickening fear. He knew what Xanthus would do to him, and he prepared for it the past two days. But death was something you could never prepare for, at least when the process would be so terrible. He awaited the words that would decide his fate.

Xanthus sighed and announced to the room with satisfaction: "You are guilty of practicing magic and treason. According to law, you will die by fire. You will be executed at dawn tomorrow."

Titus closed his amber eyes tightly with fear and furrowed his eye brows. The guards picked him up by the shoulders and dragged him out of the throne room. "You're a coward!" He shouted angrily back at the King. "At least I will die a warrior of the druid clan!" Titus was hauled out the huge throne room doors that very moment, and taken back down into the dungeons to wait for the dawn... when he would be executed.

"I wish to be alone," Xanthus ordered his crowd of watchers. "You are all dismissed until further notice." They left and Xanthus sat back down in his royal chair.

The King had not forgotten that his Queen had wanted a word with him before the trials had begun. He placed his right hand gently on the top of hers.

"You wanted to speak with me," he said with a loving smile. They had been married for years, deeply in love. Xanthus was sure she would never betray him for another man, and there was no question about it. In his opinion Anne was crazy about him, and she seemed to never leave his side. That was exactly how he felt about her.

"Yes, it... it is quite important, my love," she told him with a smile.

Xanthus placed his elbow on the arm of the black velvet chair and rested his head in the palm of his hand, his other arm spread out across his plump stomach. "Is it?" He said with an affectionate smile on his lips. "Tell me, I'm listening."

"Well," Anne smiled nervously and reached over to place a hand on her husband's chest which was heated by the sun's light. "You will be happy to hear this, I am sure."

"Out with it," he chuckled affectionately, welcoming her touch. "You have me curious now."

Queen Anne took a deep breath and smiled. "I think I am with your child," she announced to him.

He kissed her temple lovingly. "That's wonderful!" He exclaimed softly to her. After all this wait... all the druids would finally be executed and most importantly his wife would be expecting a child. He didn't know how this morning could get any better. "I love you, Anne," he whispered affectionately as he stroked her cheek with his fingers.

Titus was thrown to the hay filled ground of the prison cell roughly, skidding on the floor. The guards locked the cell door and left him in the dark. There was nothing to light the hall of prison chambers except for a couple of fiery torches. Titus rested his back up against the iron bars placed his chin on his knees, just thinking about what lay ahead of him the following dawn.

"Titus?" He heard a familiar voice speak from the cell across of him. "What did the King say?"

"What do you think he said, Avyrus?" He exclaimed with irritation. Titus was not angry at King Avyrus, just afraid. "He said exactly what he always says. Let the druid be burned at the stake!"

Avyrus was silent for a moment. The feelings that were going through him now... why couldn't he save his clan? Why did Xanthus have to be so unfeeling? Why? Avyrus wanted to let it out through tears for a moment, but he was a man. Never mind being the

King of the druid clan. He had pride to maintain. "I'm sorry, Titus," he said quietly. It was his duty to his clan to protect them and care for their well-being, and being unable to do that made him feel like a helpless child.

"Right," Titus growled.

"I mean it, Titus," the druid King pressed on. "I'm sorry that I couldn't have protected you and the others better. I'm sorry for everything that's happened to us. I take the blame."

"It's not your fault," Titus responded to Avyrus' apology. In fact, if it weren't for the wolf that Titus had brought into the clan they could have escaped much more easily. Or maybe not even be attacked in the first place. "It's mostly my fault. I brought the wolf into the clan, and we knew that Xanthus thinks wolves are a sign of sorcery. If it hadn't been for me, this probably wouldn't have even happened."

There were about ten minutes of silence before Avyrus started to feel comfortable enough to speak again. "The wolf will save our clan," he spoke with great confidence. "It is because you brought this wolf to us that we will be saved from any trouble with Xanthus forever."

Titus could not believe his ears. What had provoked Avyrus to say such a crazy thing? "Have you gone mad, sire?" He turned to look at his King through the bars, raising a brow.

"No, I have not," Avyrus responded. "One year ago, our physician Tairek gave a prophecy about the coming of a white wolf with the eyes the color of grass. He said that she would save us."

"I think you've both gone mad."

"Do not mistake Tairek's old age for weakness, young warrior," King Avyrus snapped sternly. "He has never been wrong about his prophecies before, what makes you think he'd be wrong now?"

"Because you must use logic, sire," Titus retorted. He had not mistaken Tairek's old age for weakness; he was just clearly stating that a wolf was not capable of the things Avyrus spoke of. "A wolf is just a beautiful creature. Not a hero."

CHAPTER THREE

The orange sprays of sunlight peered through the branches of the leafless trees, shining down upon Sascha's majestic snow white fur. The ground was damp with water that had formerly been frost, which the white wolf had melted with her sufficient body heat. The white she-wolf had fallen asleep very quickly, even rudely dozing off while having a conversation with Akemi, the young she-wolf that had sheltered her for the night and was going to lead her to Windstorm City that morning. Sascha didn't even open her eyes as she lay on the freezing cold leaves of the forest floor. The sun's warmth was hitting her in such a way that made her feel like she was back in the druid camp when everything was alright. Back when Sascha used to go to the Warming Stones where she would nap and let the warmth of the noon sun soak into her slick white fur, dreaming about hunting with Zachery and fetching herbs for Tairek. How she missed those days... even if Sascha was meant to save the druids from King Xanthus back in the Kingdom of Aerulis, she had a feeling that things would never be quite the same as they had been.

"Good morning, Sascha!" A female's voice disturbed her from her memories. It was Akemi, with... wait. What was that smell? Sascha knew it anywhere! It was freshly killed prey! Sascha's head then shot up and her eyes widened with excitement. Oh yes, it was not just one rabbit, it was two. She had to admit Akemi was a good hunter to have caught two rabbits in one outing... especially when it was so cold out!

"This one is for you," Akemi mumbled through fur as she placed a huge rabbit at Sascha's paws. She also noticed from the bite marks on the rabbit that Akemi had killed it with respect, delivering a very quick nip to the back of the neck. This way, the animal hadn't felt any pain. Well then, that was something new Sascha had just learned about the gray she-wolf: she respected the environment and all its living creatures, and did not kill for sport. Sascha had hunted with Zachery, but that was only to bring back food for the druid clan.

The white she-wolf began to lick at the ragged fur of the rabbit, becoming quickly hungrier than before. Her mouth watered for the rabbit's juicy meat, which she would get to in just a moment. There was something she knew she needed to say first. "Thank you, Akemi," she barked with an appreciative gleam of her eyes.

"It was no problem!" Akemi gave a bright smile at the white wolf. The light gray she-wolf looked up at the sun in an attempt to tell the time of day, and then looked down at her rabbit. "Eat up! You'll need it, you look like you've been starved."

After eating their first meal of the day and Sascha's first meal in two days, they set off to find Windstorm City like Akemi had promised the night before. It took a long walk for them to reach the other end of the Twilight Forest, which now looked like a beautiful haven for wolves in the day time.

"So how far is the village now?" Sascha asked, panting from the long walk. It was now the late afternoon, and the white she-wolf realized just how much the Twilight Forest took up of the mountainous area. Such a large amount and a vast travel distance to the lower village of Windstorm City... filled with Twilight Firs, dead leaves on the ground, and icy temperatures.

"Not much further," Akemi responded, breathing heavily in time with Sascha's. Akemi's aqua blue looked up ahead, seeing the end of the trees and a hill. "Oh, thank the Lord. I think it's just over this hill, Sascha."

"That would be nice," Sascha mumbled through the bag of coins she carried.

"It would."

Climbing up the steep grassy hill, Sascha and Akemi started to pant harder from the strain. They dug their claws in the ground to keep from sliding down and used their muscles to their advantage. It may seem like they were being over dramatic, but they were not. You would be aching too if you had been through the white she-wolf's experience.

Until finally they reached the top of the hill and gazed out upon the gigantic village and city off in the distance. It was a beautiful sight, and the King that ruled this city was lucky to have such a view from his castle. She knew from how many gold coins she had that Rei would be in the upper city, for his training would be expensive and the common man would never be able to afford it. Though ironically the common wolf would be able to afford the training; she cracked a faint smile at this thought.

"So we need to go to the upper town?" Akemi inquired, turning her blue stare from Sascha to the beautiful city.

"Yes," Sascha responded blankly, still not speaking clearly through the bag. "Akemi, do you have any idea where Rei's Quarters are?"

"Not really," Akemi replied, unhappy that she didn't have an answer for her friend. Sighing, she looked at the bag of gold that Sascha carried. "What's in that bag, by the way?"

Sascha remembered what Tairek had done for a moment, and then focused back on Akemi's question. "Five gold coins. One of the, ah... druids gave it to me."

Akemi chuckled with surprise and interest: "One of the druids gave a bag of gold to a wolf?"

Sascha's cheeks reddened. She had told Akemi everything about her situation, except for the fact that she was prophesied to save the druids and that she carried around a bag of gold. "To pay for Rei's training," she answered fairly quickly.

Akemi's chuckling started to fade away. "Well, I can see you've had that blasted thing in your mouth for days," the light gray she-wolf sympathized her, and then offered, "I wouldn't mind carrying it for a while."

Sascha shook her head in protest: "That won't be necessary."

"Oh, come now," Akemi smiled. "Besides, you're the wolf who has a relationship with the druids. You don't need a bag in your mouth the whole time."

Sascha rolled her eyes and then handed the bag to Akemi. Then they started their way toward the village of Windstorm City. Without even voicing her opinion, Sascha wondered how they would pull this off. How could they keep hidden in a village full of people who probably feared wolves? There were a couple of ways, but only one smart way. It was risky, but Sascha was well prepared to risk her life. The lower part of

Windstorm City was very clean, yet there was the occasional dirt in the road and dust on the cottages. It was very fine-looking, so she could just imagine what the upper city looked like. There probably was not a speck of dust or dirt, and the air would be as sweet as fruit.

Akemi and Sascha stalked slowly under a small bridge where a stream trickled forward, creating the peaceful ambiance of natural icy water rushing through the forest. Sascha crouched down beside the stream, her white tail resting in the chilled water. Akemi stood beside her, placing down the bag of gold.

"What do we do now?" Akemi asked the white she-wolf. She was thinking the same thing as Sascha: they would undoubtedly be shot if they showed their faces in the village. And that would just be a waste. "We need to find a way to get past the villagers without getting shot by the city officers."

Sascha sighed with frustration: "Windstorm City is a huge place. We could try to run all the way to Rei's Training Quarters, but we'd probably keel over from the strain."

Akemi laughed heartily at Sascha's response and raised a brow: "We *could* try it."

Sascha looked straight at the light gray she-wolf with a serious look on her face. "Yes, but you have to realize just how big Windstorm City is," she began. "It doesn't look like the upper city is across the street." Despite the distance, it was definitely possible... if they found a way to avoid the city officers and hide every now and then to take a rest.

"We have no choice," Akemi said calmly, "Unless, of course, you don't want to save the druids."

Sascha sighed. She didn't want to die just yet, but if she didn't try to run past the city constables then her 'family' would be executed and she would be left a coward for failing. "I'm going for it," she announced valiantly, standing up and shaking her white tail dry. Her swift movements sent freezing cold water droplets in Akemi's face, but she said nothing. The gray she-wolf just shook the water droplets from her muzzle. "Good luck," Akemi smiled.

"Thank you."

Then, Sascha took off running from behind the little stone bridge and into the streets as fast as her legs would carry her. Hearing the city officers shouting made her run faster, to a point where she thought she would place her paws the wrong way and trip. The villagers screamed, deathly afraid of the large white wolf. She could hear the city officers catching up with her on their horses, so out of pure fear Sascha made a turn down a dusty street, thus losing view of the castle in the far distance.

She ran all the way into the upper city without being caught. Sascha wondered how she did this so quickly, not even having to hide for a moment from the officers. She paid close attention to the signs on the buildings, looking for something that contained the name "Rei". All she could see so far in these clean, fruity smelling streets were taverns, blacksmith shops, fabric shops, and butcher shops; a big difference from the lower town of Windstorm. All of these shops did not matter to her, and so she continued looking hard for where Rei might be while she ran for her life. Nobles who resided in the castle of Windstorm walked these streets, and like the lower villagers they became very frightened of the quick she-wolf's appearance.

Soon, she finally spotted what she had been looking for: "Training for Gold". Could this be Rei's training? Well, she didn't really have a choice but to check it out, for the officers were going to kill her if she did not find cover soon.

Sascha leapt out of the way and toward the large wooden door of Training for Gold. She still held the little linen bag of coins and she could not let go of it, so she scratched rapidly at the door with her sharp wolf claws. It was rather loud; anyone inside would certainly hear. "Come on! Come on!" She growled with frustration. The officers had dismounted their horses and were heading straight for her!

To put things simply, a roughly scarred man opened the door and claimed the wolf to be his pet and retriever. His excuse for the bag of gold was that the she-wolf was very intelligent and would always fetch his monthly payment from the King. The guards were not idiots and they were still wondering why the man had a wolf for a pet. "It's terrifying the villagers!" One officer retorted to the young man's excuse. "The King should know about this disturbance."

"He does know about it, sir," the man gave a faint smile, scratching the back of his neck. "This guy here is used to retrieve my payments, as I stated before, so I don't have to leave while training one of my apprentices. But also to represent how strong I am, as wolves are nothing to be reckoned with."

Guy? Sascha wondered how she put up with the unintentional insults of the humans.

"The villagers of Windstorm will not appreciate a wild beast running around making trouble for them, and possibly injuring someone," another officer gave his opinion. It was then that Sascha was able to make out the scarred man's looks; he had no hair, gray eyes, and tan skin. He had many scars, ranging from face scars, shoulder and arm scars, and even scars on his scalp. She figured this was all from fighting and training. He had a fancy looking coat made of... ugh, bear skin. That was disgusting. Why did humans have to do this? Yet she was not surprised to find this out. After all, man had lost their innocence long ago. But the man also had a dark blue marking in the shape of a wolf on his right palm. It was kind of a sloppy design, actually. More like what you'd see in a cave from the ancient time. Sascha could never forget that marking though, not in a thousand years; it was a druid symbol. Had this man been a druid in the years before Sascha had been born?

The bald man thought for a moment, as if trying to figure something out or come up with an idea. "If you are at odds with me, then you are at odds with the King as well," the man responded calmly. "I command you as he commands you, so he says. You shall tell the villagers that there is nothing to worry about. Tell them that Smith here belongs to me, and is trustworthy."

Again with the male name-calling! She knew he had no idea she was a female, but it was so embarrassing being 'Smith'...

The officer in front of the man gave him an uncertain look. "Yes, sir," he dipped his head respectfully. He turned away while the rest of the guards followed, but then he looked back. "But if I hear that the animal has caused anyone trouble, I will kill it with or without the King's permission. I care too much for this city's safety for excuses." She admired this man's passion for the city of Windstorm. However, there would be no need for bloodshed anytime soon; at least not in this beautiful city.

And with that, her trouble with the city officers were over; the man led the white she-wolf inside his building. She hadn't imagined it so small! This was where the man trained his apprentices? Sascha felt bad for them, having to put up with the tiny room while handling swords and archers and every other weapon they decided to use. The back door was only twelve feet away from where she stood at the front door. Now that she thought about it, it wouldn't be possible to train people here. So where did he train them? Then it hit her... was this man Rei? Ugh, it was so obvious.

Do I lack common sense? She wondered.

"I have been trying to talk to animals lately," the man, who she presumed was the Fighting Master Rei, began calmly as he turned back to her. He went to sit on a blue velvet chair with gold arms. "I know it sounds dumb, but years ago I was able to communicate with them fluently. I've become a little rusty though."

Sascha perked her ears up; this man had the same passion to communicate with animals as the druids did... that was another hint that he might have been part of her Clan. "Were you a druid, Rei?" She barked. Would he understand her? Sascha hoped he would, for if she couldn't communicate with him then her journey would have been for nothing. Yes, she hadn't thought of the communication thing until just then. With that thought in her mind she was reminded briefly of Tairek, the man who had saved her life from the knights of

Aerulis. He had revealed to her that it was her destiny to save and protect the druids. He had also told her to go to Windstorm City to find the Fighting Master Rei, for she was not able to fight properly yet. She knew all too well that the physician was right. Sascha barely even knew how to snarl like a normal wolf.

"You... said my name," he said with surprise. So he had not fully understood her, but he seemed to be aware of her ability to speak with humans. "So you can talk. Repeat yourself!" He added with an encouraging voice.

Repeat what she had just said? "Outside I saw the palm of your hand; it had a druid symbol in the shape of a wolf!" She said, as if continuing what she had asked previously.

"Yes! Oh, I'm a bit bad at this but... I can understand everything you're saying!" He grinned.

Well, wasn't he excitable? She rolled her eyes. "Look, can you just answer me?"

"Answer what?"

"Were you a druid or were you not a druid?"

Rei raised both of his brows at her question. "I was. A very long time ago," he said simply. "But I left to become the Fighting Master of Windstorm City. It's a much better life for me. Wait, how do you know so much about the druids?"

She didn't answer his question. "Did you happen to know someone called Tairek?"

"Tairek..." Sir Rei thought for a moment. "You mean that young physician apprentice? Yes, I knew him. He was a boy when I knew him." He paused for a moment and then added in a questioning voice, "Why do you ask?"

"Because... well," Sascha began, taking a long pause. It seemed that this man had been friends with Tairek, so she did not know how to tell him of the physician's fate. "He... passed away." It was then that she saw sorrow in Rei's face. It made her a bit nervous so she added, "But he sent me here to ask kindly for your training! I can pay." She dropped the bag of gold at his feet, and he took it. He untied the tiny rope which held it tightly closed and spilled the five gold coins out. He counted the coins quickly and then lifted up his head to face her. "This will be enough," he nodded with a satisfaction.

"So, can you be more specific? I don't want to get into your business or anything, but I want to know what you plan on fighting in the future," the Fighting Master said as he stood up to grab one of his weapons. The variety of weapons he had stored in one corner of the building amazed her! It went from all kinds of swords, maces, spears, lances, shields, and even whips. It looked like he owned a torture chamber somewhere in this city. "And then I can choose the proper weapons for your training."

"The knights of Aerulis," she blurted out.

Rei gave her a look as if she were senseless. "Why would you want to do that?" He asked. "Even I don't stand a chance against them."

"I don't care if I'm killed by them, as long as the druids escape," Sascha said, and then explained what had happened to her and the druids. "That's why I need your help to defeat them."

"Well wolf, it isn't the knights that you have to worry about then," Rei said.

"I have a name you know... its Sascha," she growled, rotating her ears. "And what do mean that I don't have to worry about the knights?"

"The King of Aerulis by the name of Xanthus is the one who you need to worry about. He kills all sorcerers he can get his hands on, but it is also rumored that he practices magic himself. I can't help you with magic, but I can help you with all the fighting skills that you'll need to reach his Throne Room," Sir Rei explained carefully. The Fighting Master took out a shield with a dragon design on it and a shiny sword. She could see her white reflection in it, and it was not even blurry! Rei kept things in shape here.

Sascha wondered. If Rei had been a druid long ago, then why couldn't he help her with magic? She did not complain, though. Sascha just followed him outside to train in his huge yard which was surrounded by an iron bar fence. The grass was very green, and professionally trimmed. It made her feel bad to walk upon such nicely cut greenery, but to train with her temporary mentor she needed to do so. There were also a few bushes covered in flowers on the right side of the yard, and bushes of juniper berries on the left side.

CHAPTER FOUR

By the end of the day, Sascha had finished a round of training. She had failed big time at first, but then made up for it when she was told by Rei to summon all strength into her hind legs and then make a powerful leap into his center line. She did so, and beat him down to the ground in one swift movement of her back legs. Rei had also said that when in a real fight and using the skill that Sascha should sink her teeth into her opponent's neck flesh before even hitting the ground. That would be a killing blow for her enemies, and she was glad to have learned this helpful move. "Take heed of my word, Sascha," he had said to her. "This skill, Leap of Agrona, is only used as a last resort and it is viewed as completely disrespectful otherwise. You want to fight with honor and ability. Understand?"

"Yes, Sir Rei," she dipped her head.

And now, as she had been granted permission to do so, Sascha padded through the upper city of Windstorm to the lower town, spotting the bridge where she had left Akemi. She doubted Akemi would still be there, as she had been gone for hours. But she couldn't have strayed too far, right? It was late evening and it was hard to see, but she could just make it out.

Being half dog and all... it really ruined her chances of being a real wolf. She only had some features that wolves had, being able to see in the dark not being one of them. A dramatic wind as cold as ice suddenly stirred, waving her white fur in rhythm with the breeze. It felt nice to her, the coolness of the air reaching beneath her fur and caressing her skin. She continued walking until she made it to the little bridge, and then skidding down to the ice cold stream below that was still trickling, and would remain trickling for all of eternity. The dirt was cool, like frost. Winter was just around the corner and it should be snowing any day by now. Sascha didn't see her there, and she was not really surprised about this. Who would sit under a bridge for hours? Sascha was able to pick up Akemi's scent fairly easily, and she followed it in the opposite direction of Windstorm City until it led her back into the Twilight Forest. The evening was very beautiful; the way the breeze was cooling her of the training sweat, how the moon was full and everything was just peacefully quiet. She could hear the cicadas in the forest which relaxed her.

It had been a horrible day for Titus, knowing that he would be executed that following dawn. It would be so hot... being burned at the stake. Most of the druids had managed to fall asleep, even the ones who had been sentenced to death after him. He could not fall asleep with this in mind, and instead he attempted to find weak points in the bars for a chance at escaping. But there was no hope in that, so he just laid down for a rest. His final rest...

Surprisingly he had managed to fall asleep but at the same time he felt awake. A young maiden's soft voice woke him from his doze, while she put a key into his cell lock and opened the door slowly and soundlessly. "Hello," she said. She seemed to look scared of him, but at the same time was bracing herself to come face to face with a young druid. The maiden was carrying a plate with rice and two warm chicken legs. Why was she about to give something so fancy to him? That meal was fit for a King! She placed it down in front of him and indicated the wooden spoon that was off to the side of the platter touching the dark golden rice. Well, this was very nice of the woman... and even though he never thanked anyone for their doings, he would have to thank this young lady. He knew that she had done it at great risk to herself. "Thank you, my lady," he said while giving her a soft look. He brushed his black hair out of his eyes and grabbed one of the chicken legs, beginning to eat the first good meal that he had eaten in a few days. It was dry, but there was some bursting flavor in it. Certainly enough to excite his taste buds, especially considering he had hardly eaten lately. When he was nearly finished eating, he heard her start talking to him nervously. "I have this," she broke in, handing him a dark key. Titus looked up and saw that the key had the House of de Taske crest; the key itself was a dark greenish black, which must have been from generations of use. Aerulis had been around for nearly seven hundred years, so it was no wonder this key had lost its color and glory. Looking back to the lady, Titus tried to see what she looked like; she had beautiful, long, slightly curly light brown hair and the brightest blue eyes. "This will get you out of here. I did not want to do this at first, but... I knew I had to stop the killings of druids eventually," the young maiden went on. "Not that I'm the one who will stop it!" She corrected herself. "Your leader spoke of an animal saving the druids, no?"

"Thank you again, my lady," Titus smiled, his eyes reflecting with the real emotion of appreciation. He was truly thankful for her doing this, but just didn't know how to express it properly. "And don't believe what my King says, we all know animals can't help us. I mean, can you imagine a wolf beating up all the knights? It is completely ridiculous. Either we die or not, and I'm not afraid to die!" Titus took the old key from the woman's soft hands and, seeing that he was just about done with his food, he stood up. "I think I've memorized the palace, at least the important parts," he stared down at her. "I'm sorry; I did not get your name."

"Millie, sir," the young serving girl answered humbly. "And yours?"

"Titus, warrior from the druid clan," he smiled.

The druid warrior began to walk out of his cell, but Millie stopped him. "Titus," she started, paused, and then seeing him turn his head back to her she went on, "Come back."

He knew what she meant that that. She wanted him to stay safe, and alive. The druid rushed back to her abruptly, and kissed her quickly on the lips. "I will live," he promised her softly and then finally rushed away from her.

Out of friendliness and selfish fear, he unlocked Zachery's prison cell so that he could accompany him while he tried to find a way to get the druid clan out of the House of de Taske. Zachery was grinning as he stepped out of his cell, following at Titus' pace.

"Titus has a girlfriend," Zachery laughed heartily, but tried to keep it quiet so no one would hear them.

"Shut up," he growled in return. "Let's just get the hell out of this death trap, okay?"

The two druids, both physician apprentice and warrior, escaped with ease as they tested their magic abilities. There were two guards that were on sentry, and due to Titus' and Zachery's swift agility they were able to surround the guards with a tall ring of fire. They would never be able to leap over the scarlet flames, until of course someone came by and put the fire out.

It was a perfect trap really, and a perfect way to slip past the guards without anyone getting hurt.

It didn't take them long to find a dungeon window with bars. They used the power of force to break them, and climbed out. At this point the castle was a top a tall green hill, and luckily for them was not overlooking the kingdom of Aerulis in this direction. In fact, what they saw was overlooking their homeland; Rosewood Forest.

The two warriors dashed as far away from the Castle of Xanthus as their energy would allow them. They didn't even pay attention to their physical pain while they ran. Well, Titus didn't. He didn't know what Zachery had been feeling, but he had certainly ignored the pain. When they were a decent distance from the castle, they rested. It was conveniently on a slope, with the castle somewhat visible in the white distance. A few bright birch trees with dark brown stripes on their white bark were blocking the view, but Titus could still see it. It was taking them a while to regain their breaths, but hopefully they could set off again soon.

"Just because we've escaped doesn't mean they won't kill our clan," Zachery pointed out.

"I know," he said, standing up. "I was just about to cast a spell on Aerulis, until we come back!"

"Is that so?" Zachery inquired teasingly.

Titus was thinking about the safety of Millie just as much as he was thinking about the druid clan. He had a good idea of what the spell would be; at first it had been to cause a horrible blizzard, to delay the execution. But Titus knew that probably wouldn't work for long. Xanthus would most definitely kill them inside the dungeon if he had no other choice. And so, he decided that he would make everyone in the city of Aerulis fall into a deep sleep. It was completely harmless, and it would only last until he came back to rescue the druids.

"*Kono ōkoku wa nemuri ni ochiru*," he said, which were the ancient words for 'this kingdom will fall asleep'. As of now, hopefully, the King and all of his men and the rest of the city would be in a deep slumber.

But what would they do to rescue the druids? They hadn't really thought about that. And the only thing that they had to go on was Avyrus' insane wolf tales. The story of a white wolf that would rescue them all from death; but surely no one would believe such ridiculous nonsense!

And so the two druids set off in search of a way to save their clan. However, they did not realize just how fateful the direction they had chosen would become…

CHAPTER FIVE

"Akemi, are you out there?" Sascha's voice rang out with frustration throughout the forest. This was the Twilight Forest; it was certainly nothing to be messed with, or at least according to her new friend. She heard a twig break nearby and gasped softly in fear as it startled her. A scent came to her nose and she instantly recognized who it originated from. Sighing in relief she realized that it was Akemi's scent. Sascha had found the light gray she-wolf. Before she knew it Akemi had leapt out before her, fur bristled like needles. The white she-wolf's eyes widened and her fur stood up cold as she saw what was on her friend's body! There was a long gash stretching from above Akemi's right eye to the tip of her muzzle, dark crimson blood spilling out and staining the jet-black leaves. It was as if Sascha could see the white of the she-wolf's skull under the wound! It disturbed her how deep the cut was.

The light gray female just stood there, panting and all four legs separated with a good distance between them as if to support her balance. That wasn't all! There were four long stripes down her hip, also with blood escaping from them. "What happened?" She asked shakily, her heart pounding in her stomach. She was very deeply worried for Akemi. Who had done this? Had it been a hunter from Windstorm City? Had it been an animal? Or worse, had it been one of the magical creatures that were rumored to roam these forests at the time of twilight…? It was something much more dangerous than a hunter, because the wounds were, as she looked closer, not made by a human. The poor girl, her entire face was bleeding!

"A creature," she whispered out, trying not to strain herself too hard. "It attacked…" Akemi then winced in pain and fell to the ground. *What now?* Sascha wondered desperately in fright. *Is the creature still around?*

A loud roar that was similar to that of rough thunder was heard throughout the entire forest. Without warning a large dragon descended as quickly as the element of lightning from the tree tops. Sascha didn't even have time to scream, for the dragon had Akemi tightly gripped in its dagger sized teeth. Akemi couldn't have run before she was picked up because she was so weak from the last attack that the flying creature had given her. Sascha only snapped back to reality when the dragon started the fly up and out of the forest, carrying Akemi's poor torn body with it. Taking her friend away from her! Oh, the sight of this just made her… well, just a little pissed off.

While the dragon was flying over the tree tops to the south of Windstorm City, the white she-wolf took off as fast as her paws would carry her in an attempt to try to stop the magical animal. Sascha could remember the last time she had run like this; it was when the forest had been lit on fire by the Knights of Aerulis. Back when Tairek was alive! At this moment while trying to save her friend, she could almost feel Tairek's presence with her as she pounded the earth with her paws. She would not lose a friend this time!

Sascha thought her heart, lungs, and mind would explode; she was pelting at her full speed. She saw a black clearing, somehow unlit by the moonlight, up ahead. The clearing also meant that she'd be able to save her friend.

She knew nothing about dragons or their weaknesses, but she put that off and focused on the moment. What could she do? It wasn't that high off the ground, she could possibly leap and cling onto the thing. A white wolf with peculiar orange stripes and amber eyes leaped out of the bushes, sensing the distress. With tremendous power in his back legs the strange wolf shot upwards toward the dragon and amazingly clung on with its fangs.

Then two other wolves streamed into the clearing while the dragon was flying around, one with black fur and red swirly markings and another with white fur and ice blue stripes.

Not wanting to waste time, Sascha rushed forward and summoning all the power into her legs she took a huge leap. Due to the heavy weight of the clinging wolves the dragon was forced lower to the ground, giving Sascha a better advantage. She felt her paws meet the dragon's back, the wind made from its gigantic wings almost throwing her off balance. Immediately the white she-wolf sunk her fangs into the dragon's large shoulder. Her teeth met the shoulder bone, and the dragon let out a loud snarl mumbled out by Akemi's squealing body. A bit of blood spilled from the wound that Sascha had given the dragon and tasted strange on her tongue, but she didn't care. But no matter how hard she bit into the shoulder bone, on the verge of breaking it, the dragon would not let Akemi out of its grasp.

The white furred male with orange stripes climbed swiftly up the dragon's rib cage and came to stand by Sascha, his long claws digging into its skin. Somehow it just wasn't hard for the wolf to cling on. It seemed like it was a natural skill for him. "Stay back!" He warned sternly, and then leapt to stand perfectly between the dragon's head and Sascha. "This is far too dangerous for you."

Sascha let go of her grip on the dragon's shoulder. "Don't ever tell me what's too dangerous!"

The dragon suddenly threw itself into the surrounding trees in an attempt to throw the wolves off. The Twilight

Firs crashed to the ground with a deafening sound, followed by the beast's violent roar. The orange and white wolf did not lose his footing, and neither did the other two wolves lose their grip on its arm and chest.

The white and orange wolf turned to her angrily. "Leave!" He snarled. "We will take care of this. We will save your friend, I promise you that!"

Of course Sascha didn't plan on leaving, but before she knew it the dragon had lifted off the ground and was starting to fly upward. Slipping as the dragon flew higher and higher, she clamped onto the base of its right wing with her teeth. Even being in this type of danger she did not regret not leaving when she had the chance. She couldn't look at the dragon's head from this angle, only watch as the beast flew higher above the Twilight Forest.

"Retreat warriors retreat!" The white furred male with orange stripes yowled. Those cowards! The dragon was going somewhere, and they didn't have the guts to find out where? Well, who needed them! She was doing just fine before they showed up.

"Talomi, Strawberry!" The stern wolf began. "Jump, we'll be able to land safely in the trees!"

What kind of wolves were they, thinking that they'd survive that fall? Forgetting about them for a moment, she struggled to get a grip on the dragon's skin so that she could climb onto its back again. Instead she slipped again and then caught the dragon's arm with her fangs and wrapped her paws around it. She could see Akemi from here being tightly carried in the beast's mouth. "Sascha, help me!" She heard her friend scream just before Sascha was thrown with great force down toward the ground. It was a long, lingering fall that filled her with dread, but she did not scream as she plummeted down. She was just too shocked.

A pair of teeth bit into the nape of her neck and suddenly she was on the ground. The impact from hitting the ground had only hurt her hip because her upper body was elevated, but it wasn't terribly painful. She doubted it was even broken. Sascha's upper body dropped and she felt the shock grow stronger as she laid there. She didn't know, but it was probably the shock that caused her to lose consciousness.

"Hey, you're awake!" A black she-wolf's voice said excitedly as Sascha opened her eyes slowly, only to close them again as she slipped back into unconsciousness. It could have been seconds later or it could have been hours later, but she opened her eyes again. Her eye lids were heavy, and it was a struggle to keep them open at all.

"Welcome back," a male voice greeted her neutrally. She weakly looked over at her right side and saw the white male wolf with orange stripes. "Glad to see you're okay, she-wolf."

"Yeah," she whispered, not fully comprehending what he had said. She was in a large cave lying on her side. There were many crevices in the silver wall of the cave, and the sprays of sunlight seemed to peak shyly through the lichen that hung over the entrance of the cave. Her head hurt a bit, but it was quite easy to ignore. It didn't hurt that much. Then she remembered with a sensation of horror; Akemi had been taken by that damn dragon! "Akemi, where is she?" She jolted up to a sitting position. Trying to stand, she added to the orange and white male, "You said you'd rescue her!" Of course, she had forgotten that they had jumped off the dragon before getting to her gray friend.

"I'm sorry, young she-wolf. We didn't have a chance to rescue her this time," the male responded simply. "But we won't let Harloc kill your friend. I made a promise and I intend to keep it."

Akemi was still in danger? Who was Harloc? "But… you… what are we waiting for, then?" Sascha snapped. "Go and get your reinforcements or something so we can go and fight this Harloc!"

"It's not that simple," the black she-wolf with red swirly markings said. This female was the one whose voice she had first awoken to. The female had very pretty aqua blue eyes. "We decided that we must tell our pack alpha about this. The only reason we want to rescue your friend from The Horde is because we know that the prophecy cannot be fulfilled without her."

Sascha narrowed her green eyes with wonder. Did Akemi also have a prophecy? "What prophecy?"

CHAPTER SIX

"So, you're trying to tell me that it's my destiny to save the Twilight Pack from Harloc?"

"Technically yes," the black she-wolf, whose name was Strawberry, answered. "That is the reason we're helping you. We also know that the druids have been prophesying you for a while now."

"What do you know about the druids?" Sascha flattened her ears. What kind of wolves were these? They seemed to know many things.

"We receive dreams just like the druids do," Orion, the orange and white wolf, replied. "Anyway, enough talk. For this prophecy to fulfill itself, we must rescue Akemi from Harloc."

"Alright," Sascha flattened one of her ears. "Explain to me something. If you think Akemi is an important wolf of prophecy, then why do you have to ask your alpha's permission? Doesn't he want you to rescue her?" Orion had earlier mentioned that they had to ask their alpha's permission.

"To be honest with you, Akemi was a former Twilight Pack omega," Strawberry answered. "Thor was forced to exile her under the impression that she had killed the pack's beta; murder being one of the most horrid actions. We see it as an abomination. But we have proof that she did not."

Sascha tilted her head. "So then if Thor thinks she did kill your pack's beta, then why would he want to help her escape Harloc?"

"We use the proof we have, and hope Thor believes us and gives us reinforcements to fight against Harloc."

"Well, then," Sascha shot up to all four paws, claws digging into the cave floor excitedly. "Let's hurry!" The white she-wolf pelted through the lichen entrance and into the pack's clearing. Strawberry and Orion followed Sascha, coming to stand beside her.

The pack was distracted from their daily duties by Sascha's sudden appearance. They shot her cold and suspicious glares, their tails waving to and fro with tension. One wolf, a very unusual looking gray wolf with green stripes and red eyes, stalked toward her with a menacing snarl on her lips. "Ignore Okina, she just wants to protect her pack," Orion touched Sascha's shoulder with the tip of his tail, and then waved it toward a huge cave on the other side of the camp. It had a long, lush lichen curtain hanging over the entrance. The rock cave went up like a mountain, but it was obvious that it sloped downward on the other side. "That's where Thor makes his den," he went on and beckoned for Sascha and Strawberry to follow.

The three wolves stood in front of the den entrance. "Well, this is it," Strawberry announced.

"I can smell you, Orion and Strawberry," the voice said. The white she-wolf presumed it was Thor, the Twilight Pack alpha. She was eager to speak with him, wondering if he'd be generous enough to spare a few of his warriors to fight Harloc, the Dragon Lord of Doragontaigun. "Come in, I can tell you need to tell me something."

"Good luck," Sascha said, and watched the two wolves go in. She followed them, pushing through the damp lichen. Shaking the pale green lichen from her face she looked up and saw the Twilight Pack alpha. What she saw certainly impressed her; the rest of the pack seemed to be lean and skinny with unbelievable strength and skills, but Thor was a gigantic male. He was muscular and fierce looking, with a large patch of his fur, probably about eleven inches of it, bitten and clawed off. His fur was almost spiky, as if frozen in place with ice. Thor's pelt was a handsome shade of dark butterscotch brown with three darker stripes on his back, pale underfur, and blue eyes. His welcoming glare shifted from Orion and Strawberry to Sascha, his stare then becoming stony. "Who is this?" He asked with a low growl.

"This is Sascha, sir," Strawberry answered the strong alpha. The white wolf sincerely hoped he wouldn't engage in a fight with her for whatever reason. She hardly doubted she'd live, never mind win. "She would like to speak with you."

Wait, I have to ask him for help? She wondered with disbelief. Forcing hesitation to leave her, Sascha stepped forward to face him directly. She kept a firm glare with the powerful alpha. "I wish to ask you, Thor, for reinforcements," she began. He pulled away from her gaze and let out a loud snarl. She expected him to say something and waited for a moment, but he never did. Therefore, she went on, "I wish to ask you for reinforcements… to fight against Harloc of the Doragontaigun Horde. A friend of mine, Akemi, has been taken prisoner by the dragon lord."

"Did you just say Akemi?" Thor yelled, his fur bristling with fury. "You must be one of her little minions! I always knew she'd betray us to Harloc. I would never risk my warriors over a disgusting traitor like her."

Sascha growled with anger at the way Thor so openly insulted her friend. Who the hell did he think he was?

"I'll handle this, Sascha," Orion stepped forward to face his alpha. "It's the truth, sir. We were there to fight one of Harloc's underlings, and it was indeed Akemi the dragon was carrying."

"It's not that I don't believe it was Akemi," Thor gave a sharp growl at the warrior. "I just refuse to help her.

And I refuse to believe you have any real proof that Akemi didn't kill Python."

Orion sighed and then shot Strawberry a worried look. The orange striped male looked back at the pack alpha once the black she-wolf dipped her head with the same emotion of worry. "You're right, sir," he began with his ears flattened and head down. "We do not have the proof, even if we said we did. But we do have a better solution."

Sascha pricked her ears; so they hadn't had the proof the whole time? This attempt was just going nowhere, especially with a Pack alpha like Thor.

"What could that possibly be?" Thor grumbled with annoyance. "If you are trying to convince me, you're wasting your time. And how could I trust my warriors if they keep up defending a murderer?"

"Please, sir, take the time to listen to what I need to say," Orion pleaded, and waited for his alpha to say something. When nothing came out of Thor's mouth, the young warrior went on, "It all began when I had gone to sleep one night. It wasn't long after you'd banished Akemi from the Twilight Pack. I had a dream that Python came to me and told me that Akemi was innocent, and in fact Harloc was responsible for his death. He said that Harloc just wanted to stir up trouble within the Pack, and blaming Akemi would certainly destroy a prophecy or two."

Was Thor beginning to see reason now? She hoped so. It looked like it, considering how he hadn't interrupted his warrior. Strawberry stepped forward. "You've heard of the druids, right?" She asked softly. "Well, they prophesied the coming of a great white wolf with the eyes of grass, did they not? Well, this she-wolf stands before you now. And you care so much about druid prophecy? Then you will have to rescue Akemi, or that prophecy will be ruined forever. And we'll never be freed from Harloc."

"Shut your amateur mouth!" Thor snarled viciously, his canine fangs seeming to be as sharp as ever. The points of those fangs barely missed Strawberry's muzzle, but she forced herself not to flinch from her Pack alpha. "You think it's so easy? I let this she-wolf take control of my warriors and you go and kill Harloc, just like that? It's not that easy! Harloc is an Ituic Dragon! He is a rare species of dragon that is rumored to be very tolerable to battle wounds. Almost as if he were immortalized, even though everyone has their weaknesses... not even a dragon his size could inflict a decent wound on him without getting killed in the process, so they say."

Sascha needed to say something here. Anything, for she was getting a bit worried that Thor wouldn't quit having a negative mindset. "Thor, look. If you don't believe Akemi is worth saving, then would you please find it essential to save me the trouble of rescuing her myself?"

Thor narrowed his eyes at her. "That would be suicide."

"I know, but… like Strawberry said. I was prophesied by the druids about a year ago," she began to explain. "I am supposed to save them from being executed at the hands of King Xanthus of Aerulis. And I fear without a friend by my side to support me, I might never be able to win." She was partly trying to play on his heart strings with the sappy she-wolf talk.

Thor sighed stressfully. "I know that, Sascha. But can you really expect me to send my warriors off to die? I can't betray them like that," he spoke casually, but also with a deep emotion of grief in his eyes.

"I understand, Thor," Sascha dipped her head respectfully to the leader. She could see what he was feeling, not wanting his warriors to die at the hands of Harloc. "But if you don't try, then when will your pack ever be freed from Harloc's grasp?"

He gave no reply, just sat down in silence.

"Perhaps we could talk it over with your pack members? See what they want to do," Sascha suggested with a humble voice.

"I'm afraid they'd make a decision they'd live to regret."

"But their deaths wouldn't be in vain. They'd die protecting their Pack. Although I can assure you I will not let them die."

It took Thor a while to respond, as if he were deep in thought. "You have my permission to ask my Pack to fight."

"Thank you, sir," Sascha smiled gratefully. "I know how much your Pack means to you, I promise you I won't let so much as a scratch appear on their bodies."

Giving Thor a respectful dip of her head, she turned and headed for the exit of the Alpha's den. A sharp growl made her turn back to the pack leader. "Sascha, I trust you with my pack," he snarled warningly. "If I see so much as a scratch on them when they come back, if they come back at all, then you know to expect I will spill your blood over the stones for it."

These words from the alpha chilled her to the bones, and it made her wonder. What if she failed him? What if they all died in battle with Harloc? But then she realized something; she realized that she could not lose this fight. If she did, then everything would be ruined; her plans for saving the druids, rescuing Akemi, everything. It would all disappear. She could not afford to die yet. "I assure you, Thor," Sascha gave him a serious look. "I assure you that I will not let anyone die by the fire of Harloc. His reign is over." It was just completely and simply over. Without waiting for his reply, or for Strawberry and Orion to follow, she left the den and entered the clearing. Looking around for perhaps a ledge or a higher place to address the Twilight Pack, she lashed her tail with anticipation. This was an urgent message she needed to give to these wolves. It was only a matter of time before Harloc would kill Akemi, and then everything would have been for nothing. Then she saw a ledge just above the alpha's den entrance. She padded toward it and quickly accessed the ledge by leaping up onto a boulder and then onto the mossy location above the entrance. Without her having to say anything, the wolves gathered below. Anger and tension was radiating from them, something that Sascha hoped wouldn't prove to be too much trouble.

"What is this intruder doing up there?"

"That isn't Thor!"

They seemed like they were ready to rip her fur off. But the white she-wolf tried to ignore their faces and comments. "Thor has given me permission to address you," she began, and waited a moment to see if they'd say anything. When they didn't, she just explained everything that had previously happened with Akemi and of her decision to go and fight Harloc.

"And you expect us to go and die?"

"No, I don't expect you to do that," she responded. "I won't let a scratch get on your pelt."

"How do we know that?"

"Yes! How do we know that you'll keep us alive and well?"

"Why can't Thor just lead us into battle?"

"Don't be an idiot! He'd never be so stupid. And who said we're going anyway?"

"*Attention!*" Sascha growled sternly. "You all have experienced Harloc's wrath, have you not?" She wanted an answer from them, hoping that it would help them believe she was here to help, not lead them to their deaths. They all acknowledged the fact that Harloc had been tormenting them for years, one way or another. With that down, they needed to get somewhere in this Pack meeting. "You have all heard of the druids. They prophesied me. I am supposed to save the druid clan from the hands of King Xanthus of Aerulis. I can assure you that I will not let any of you die. I promise." She let a moment of silence pass, so it could register in their heads. A ripple of agreement rose from all of the Pack members. She was surprised to hear them all agree with her! In a voice of authority, she went on with query. "Do any of you know where Harloc makes his home?"

"In the Meadows of Agrona," a young Twilight Pack wolf responded. "It is not a meadow, but instead a strange barren land. It's a scary place, full of animal skeletons as well as those of the humans."

"Do you know how to get there?" Sascha asked the male wolf.

"Of course," he replied. "See those mountains?" Sascha turned to see the mountains that the wolf had indicated. "He and his horde are just over those."

"Good," she murmured to herself, giving a faint smile. She would lead her platoon over the mountain, and greet Harloc with a deafening blow. How exciting to shed a villain's blood! "I have a feeling that Harloc is increasing power by putting other dragons under his command, planning to destroy us and Windstorm. But we cannot stop him alone! We need more warriors. I will give you one week!"

One week was a short time, and so the Pack protested with disbelief. "I'm sorry, but we have no time!" Sascha announced over the voices. "I will separate the Twilight Pack into two groups. I will lead one to the north. The other, Orion will lead into the west. Gather as many skilled warriors that are willing to fight against Harloc and the rest of Doragontaigun as quickly as you can! We will meet here in one week!"

Howls of agreement rose from the wolves, and she yelled over them to give a final order. "The time to set off is now! When we return to camp, the war will begin and we shall make the mountains shake to their core!"

Orion emerged from the Alpha's den and took the wolves into his own group. Sascha leaped down and separated wolves into her group. So now, each platoon leader had the equal amount of warriors. The time to leave was now, and so they did so; Orion led his warriors to the west as ordered, and Sascha lead her platoon to the north. They would gather many wolves and possibly dogs to fight against Harloc. And so, just like that, Sascha's true courage began to show.

They had spread out over England. The two platoons had gathered many wolves and dogs to join their cause. Sascha had no way of knowing if Orion was doing well in the quest for more warriors. But at least when they got back she'd have many warriors to fight against Harloc, whether Orion's platoon did or not. Talomi, the white wolf with icy blue stripes who had fought one of Harloc's minions, had helped advise her in the leadership of the group. And so, she'd made him her second in command. They'd gone from kingdom to kingdom looking for recruits. It all burned in their hearts to find enough warriors to fight Harloc and win. Sascha's blood as a wolf burned at the thought of gathering all the warriors to fight against the dragon. She was filled with warm memories of Zachery and the druids.

They'd recruited over fifty warriors, on occasions gathering entire wolf packs or feral dog groups. These groups far and wide had been affected by Harloc and his horde. So therefore they'd joined Sascha's platoon.

The white she-wolf prayed that Orion was having the same luck as she was having. A couple of dogs in particular stood out in the group that was well into the fifties and counting. Chino, a male Neapolitan mastiff, was very strong and committed to killing Harloc. Upon Sascha and the platoon meeting him, he'd been a feared rogue in the kingdom of Brighton. Sascha and Talomi had explained to him what they were doing in Brighton, that they had been gathering enough warriors to defeat Harloc and how he seemed just right for the job. She'd told him to think about the offer, but he'd just left without saying a word. He'd showed his strength when a hunter had found the group making temporary camp in the forest, suddenly appearing from the bushes and attacking the man with incredible strength. He had decided to join the group, and Sascha was glad for his support. Another dog was an Irish wolfhound whose name was Adam. He'd actually been a hunting dog before Sascha had been able to convince him to join her platoon. The two were both amazing fighters. It was almost time to meet up with Orion's group, so Sascha was glad to have recruited them into her numbers before the time was up.

Sascha knew very well that Harloc could have eaten Akemi by now, and the thought made her stomach sick, but she had no other choice but to go looking for other dogs and wolves to fight by her side. There was no chance in the world that she could beat a dragon and his entire horde alone and single pawed.

That night the group slept under the stars. It was a very beautiful clearing, similar to the one in the mystical Twilight Forest. But Sascha could not sleep, she was restless. She sat upon a tall boulder that rested in the center of the snowy clearing, knowing that when the platoon reunited with Orion's, they would be heading for what could be a fatal battle. She knew for a fact that many of the warriors could die, despite her promise of their survival. But she had to serve them as a good leader, especially in battle. How could she go into war with Harloc knowing that most of those loyal Twilight Pack warriors wouldn't be coming back alive? Or those loners, some of them wouldn't be able to return to their old lives again?

"Sascha...?"

The white she-wolf was surprised when she heard a strange voice behind her. She whipped around and saw that Adam, the male Irish wolfhound, had called upon her. "Adam," Sascha greeted with a dip of her head, and then asked, "What is it?"

Adam climbed up the rock that the platoon leader was sitting on and sat down beside her, looking at the beautiful white moon. The moon reminded Sascha of the night Akemi had been abducted, the evening she'd just gotten back from training with Rei the

Fighting Master. Certainly it was not enough training to help her fight King Xanthus, never mind Harloc? "I think you're worried about the battle," Adam told her.

"How did you guess?" Sascha inquired somewhat sarcastically.

"I have a tendency to know when others are stressed, and the rest was just a lucky guess," he chuckled with friendliness in his deep voice. His pale gray fur blew in the sudden breeze. "I was part of a pack of feral dogs once. Harloc was the one who killed them all. I was lucky enough to escape with my life. I've hated him ever since. So I intend to serve your pack to the best of my ability."

"I thank you for your loyalty, Adam," she sniffed the air. "It's kind of cold tonight; you should probably get some rest with the others. We will be leaving tomorrow."

"What about you?" Adam asked, though still stood up as if he were going to leave her. It had snowed only a few days into the journey, so the snow was still hard and freezing on the ground... which made it even colder out.

"I'll go to bed soon."

CHAPTER SEVEN

The platoon streamed into the camp like millions of ants, except their numbers weren't nearly that many... unfortunately. It looked like Orion's group had already arrived, and that his platoon's numbers had significantly grown since their last meeting a week before. Sascha had led her own platoon of over fifty canines for two days practically nonstop to get there. That completed the week cycle. She was proud that Orion had gathered so many warriors.

Sascha's group stopped and rested at one side of the Twilight Pack's clearing, and then Orion's did the same thing on another side of the clearing. The white she-wolf's platoon was extremely exhausted, their gasps and groans and howls of soreness sounding loudly over the Twilight Pack Clearing. She'd pushed them hard upon returning to camp. She wondered if they'd be able to start the battle today! Sascha raced off from her group to Orion's, and immediately spotted him in the shade of a Twilight Fir. "Orion," she greeted him. "How did your week go?"

"It went fine," he answered with exhaustion. "We recruited over one hundred warriors."

"Wow, that's impressive!" Sascha exclaimed. "My platoon only recruited about fifty warriors. So in total we got approximately one hundred and fifty to join our cause, that's very good." Not to mention the other thirty Twilight Pack members. That was a huge army of wolves and dogs!

"Listen up!" Sascha heard the Twilight Pack Alpha call out sternly. It was time. The war would begin soon. The pack of nearly two hundred gathered tiredly below the Alpha's Ledge that was just above the den, where Sascha had stood and announced the gathering of recruits for the war against Harloc. "The time has come, my pack. This is your last chance to retreat from this cause. Once you cross over the mountain, you will be in Harloc's Land. You won't be able to turn back from there."

The alpha let the words sink into his pack and the other recruits. Sascha wondered if any of the wolves would back off and run away. She wouldn't have called them a coward if they had. In fact, it would have been a wise decision. Before she knew it, the Twilight Pack alpha spoke again as Talomi and Orion came to sit beside her. "Sascha and Talomi, my beta male, will lead you all into battle." Talomi puffed up his white and ice blue striped fur with excitement. Sascha was happy for him; he'd be leading the pack into battle alongside her. But she also felt bad that Orion hadn't been chosen to lead along with them. He had done a lot of work, getting those one hundred recruits. "I think that was a good choice, Talomi," she told him, referring to what Thor had decided upon who should lead the gigantic platoon of canines.

"My dearest Twilight Pack," Thor began bitterly, addressing only his pack. "Remember, this is your choice. It is not mine. If any of you die, do not blame me. In fact, I wanted to stop you from joining this battle. This is a suicide mission, I hope you know that!"

Sascha heard no voices after that. No responses to their alpha. It looked like no one thought it right to leave their mission to kill Harloc. The white she-wolf looked up to Thor, and saw something in his eyes. Sadness...? Or perhaps it was more like a troubled look? She couldn't exactly tell because she was not close enough. But she knew that the alpha was not enjoying having to watch his pack go off to war.

Sascha stepped forward and stood directly below the Alpha's Ledge. "We must go now," she told them all. "Akemi needs to be rescued, and Harloc needs to be put to rest once and for all."

Howls and cries of agreement rose loudly once she'd finished. It was nearly as loud as thunder on a horrible stormy night. Sascha was surprised Harloc didn't hear them and swoop over the mountains to kill them. It was time to put an end to the Twilight Pack's seemingly endless misery.

She led them over the mountains, marching in place like soldiers going off to war. Talomi padded hard in place beside her at the head of the platoon, his head held high with pride. Talomi's amber eyes glowed with vanity, and he held his ice blue striped tail straight out like a point. Sascha's eyes did not contain any emotion and she brushed away the feeling of fear to prevent the other wolves from smelling her burning fear. Her fur lay flat against her back, and her tail was kind of drooping low. She did not have the pride and glory that Talomi was feeling as he led the pack over the mountain. She still worried that they might not be coming back alive after the battle with Harloc.

They were almost in Harloc's Land which was located on the other side of the mountain. She could smell the smoke, the horrible smell of smoke that took her back to the night that Tairek died and the druids were captured. It seemed like she'd forgotten about them and was focusing more on a dumb pack of wolves. But then again she was not doing that, she was going to rescue her friend from a blood-hungry dragon that ruled this part of Great Britain. Letting her heart sink deeper into the thought of what she should be doing right now, she felt fear and guilt. What if the druids had been killed by now? What if she'd failed them and her prophecy? Tairek would have died for nothing! But what choice did she have? Sascha had to help these wolves especially now after gathering so many recruits. And she definitely couldn't leave Akemi to die.

"We descend from here," Talomi called out over the giant platoon, distracting Sascha from her thoughts. They were there so soon? It seemed like only minutes ago they had been standing in the Twilight Pack Clearing, listening to Thor's speech to the platoon. She guessed it was true. Time did fly when you were just thinking. Out of curiosity the white she-wolf looked out from the top of the mountains into Harloc's Land, and she could hardly believe what she saw there. The land had many cracks in it, there were no trees, and there were a few tar pits with animal skeletons stuck in them. There was no snow, probably because the dragons had burned it all. It was a wasteland! How could anyone, even a dragon, possibly survive here? There certainly wasn't any prey. But then Sascha realized something...one of the reasons Harloc terrorized the animals outside of his Lands was possibly because he needed to eat. Of course! He hunted those on the outside, and brought them back and killed them for his food. Even if those animals were wolves. She felt sick at the thought of Akemi being eaten...

"Remember what Thor said, this is your last chance to turn your back on this battle. We cannot afford to have cowards with us," Talomi continued loudly so that every wolf and dog may hear him. Sascha noticed that a few of the recruits ran away, turning their backs on the upcoming battle. That was wise of them, she supposed. Adam and Chino were still with the platoon though and had not run away. She hadn't expected them to run away; they seemed like strong and brave warriors. She hoped that none of them would lose their lives in the battle that was to come.

"I will take that as a sign that you are all ready," Talomi yelled out over the platoon and then turned to Sascha. "You give the signal for us to move out."

She nodded and then looked around for a place she could tower over the gigantic pack to give the command to move downward. She saw a bit of a hill to her left and climbed up it. Sascha was now looking out over the pack that was expecting to hear the words that would command them to descend to battle. "All wolves and dogs, listen to me!" She stated deafeningly. "This is a battle that must be fought... to save Akemi, and to restore your freedom! Move out, now!"

The canines howled with agreement. When Sascha reached the head of the platoon again, they rushed down the high mountain. The wolves caused tremors to go through the earth, their paws hitting the dirt hard. It was both like an earthquake, and a warning of their presence. Harloc and his Doragontaigun Horde would for sure feel the trembling in the mountains. She wondered what would be waiting for them when they reached the ground and were out of the mountains.

After about fifteen minutes they had reached the bottom of the mountain and had entered Harloc's Land. Talomi was still beside her and she turned to him, her black nose sniffing the air. "The air doesn't smell of dragon. I can't pick up one trace of it," she told him. "Organize the platoon. Make sure they are aligned properly, like a King would order his knights to do." The ground was so hot! It was obvious that the dragons burned their own territory to keep it at a bearable temperature for themselves but anything else that strayed into their territory would die from the heat! The wolves were starting to sweat, but being as big as they were they probably would not die from the extreme temperatures. After all, the wolves still had the winter breeze to cool them off.

"Nothing's happening," Talomi whispered to her, disappointment in his voice.

She didn't reply. She was busy looking around for any movement. But Talomi was right, nothing was happening. "I wonder what's..." she trailed off as she began to see a dust tornado rushing toward them. It was almost as big as the mountain in back of them. Glowing blue lines encircled the dust tornado, along with many strange symbols.

"What is that?" A random dog came to stand beside her, ears rotated backward with fear. The dog was right! What could it possibly be? Then the dust cyclone stopped directly in front of them.

"Why do you enter my Land?" The big dust storm spoke, its voice louder than the loudest thunder, as if it were a god. It forced everyone to crouch down with horror from the sheer start. "ANSWER ME!" The voice of the twister added, seeming so loud it could shake the earth to its core. There were then whimpers of terror all around her, even from Talomi.

Sascha only did what her instincts told her to do next. "We are here to take back our freedom! We are here to rescue my friend from Harloc!"

"Why if it isn't Sascha, the little white pipsqueak," the dust cloud spoke harshly. "I have been waiting for your arrival for hundreds of years. At last you have come." And then the cloud disappeared into thin air, causing an uprising of dust everywhere you looked. Wait... this cloud wasn't just a normal talking dust cloud. It was Harloc! Sascha knew it by the way he acted, though she'd never even met him before.

Suddenly the dust cleared and she saw dragons closing in on the platoon quickly in the distance. They were silhouettes in the now dusty barren lands, but she knew they were coming for them. When they were so close Sascha could almost leap forward and touch them, she gave the go ahead. "Spread out and attack as many of them as you can!" She yelled quickly.

She raced straight forward at one of the dragons and just in time remembered what to do. Sascha copied what Master Rei had taught her back in Windstorm City, and relocated all the power into her back legs. With that, the brave white she-wolf took a massive leap upward and unsheathed her claws. Her long white fangs seemed to extend forward like a shark's as she opened her mouth. Sascha sank her pointed white teeth into the dragon's abdominal area, soon feeling the warm blood gush out of the wound. It soaked her down from her chin to the tip of her tail, vibrant red against her snow white coat. In the heat of the battle, she was enjoying this. Inflicting wounds on the dragon, feeling the blood soak her fur. She didn't want to sound violent, but when anyone was in battle they usually enjoyed the glory of winning. But they were far from winning at the moment. She looked up quick enough to see a hand full of claws the size of swords coming down on her, and she leaped away. This was her first battle… and it felt absolutely great!

Luckily she had dodged the dragon's fist full of claws, now she had to act quickly. She ran around to the other side of the dragon as quickly as she possibly could and then leaped up into the air. She bit into the dragon's thigh, her fangs going deeper this time. Blood welled from the wound a lot more than the one that Sascha had inflicted on the dragon's abdominal area.

It could only have been three seconds before the dragon reached its head back, razor sharp teeth coming straight down at her. She did not have enough time to react before the teeth closed in around her sides, thankfully the teeth did not go in too deep. It pulled her trying to dislodge her from the dragon's thigh. Out of pure instinct the she-wolf let go so that she would not be shredded. But she was now being shaken like a helpless kitten in the jaws of the murderous reptile! She screamed in pain, it's sword like teeth were putting a large amount of pressure on her lungs, but were not piercing them. The pain was almost unbearable for her, but she was a warrior; she had to stay strong and angry during this fight. And she would do so if it was the last thing she did!

The dragon twisted its neck around and then threw her forward, into the air. The white she-wolf thrashed in the air as she came crashing to the hot ground. Her body kicked up dust as she skidded over ten feet of battle field. Moaning with pain and shock, she struggled shakily to get up onto her paws. She was bleeding heavily from both of her sides, and every time she breathed it caused a significant amount of pain in that area. Had it punctured her lungs? When she looked up for the dragon she'd been fighting, it had already disappeared. How unfortunate! She had wanted to completely defeat him.

Sascha looked around the battlefield to check up on everything that was going on. She was shocked to see the bodies of her warriors lying on the ground in pools of their own blood, and some of that blood was dragon blood fortunately. The platoon had killed one dragon so far, and its body lay like a mountain in the middle of the battle. Some of her warriors had died already! Her fears seemed to be coming true, and she did not know what to do about it. Sascha panicked. What if she had led them all to their death?

"Sascha!" She heard a voice call to her over the howling and roaring. It was Talomi! She turned around and saw him running up behind her. Soon they were nose to nose.

"How is the battle going?" She asked her war partner quickly. To get the battle status would be a very helpful thing, and very useful.

"Many have died," Talomi answered, then pushed her down to the ground as a dragon attempted to swoop down and carry them off. They didn't want that happening again like it had with Akemi.

"Thank you," Sascha said to him gratefully.

"We need to attack more dragons!" Talomi growled fiercely and then pelted away toward a smaller dragon with a cluster of dogs fighting against it. She followed him close behind as they raced to their friends' aid. To her, this was another opportunity to kill a dragon.

The male white and icy blue striped wolf leaped up higher than Sascha ever could, his fangs bared like Harloc himself. He snarled as he flew through air, his claws unsheathed and aimed for the dragon's huge eyes. Talomi's claws raked across the tender eyes of the dragon, ultimately blinding it. It roared in pain, and dropped down to all fours. Sascha leaped up and sank her teeth into the dragon's snout, blocking the nostril airways. Dragons did not know how to breathe through their mouth, so this was a very important move for the she-wolf. The dragon swung its head back and forth, to and fro, shaking her and trying to get her off. But she refused to let go of her grasp on the opponent.

Talomi came out of nowhere and bit into the dragon's horn that was on the back of the head, instantly twisting and snapping it off. He was a natural warrior! Talomi hit the ground perfectly on his paws, half of the dragon horn being firmly held in his mouth like a dog holding its bone. The dragon spread out its wings and as quickly as it could it fled from the battle, trying desperately to get rid of the warrior dogs that clung to it.

Sascha let go of her grasp on the dragon's nostrils, leaping down to the ground and landing quite easily on her paws. There were still wolves fighting on the battlefield, but now it was another dragon down. Seeing the defeated reptile fly away in fear, looking for a place to lick its wounds, Sascha felt very proud of herself. She had defeated a dragon with the help of the pack.

King Xanthus could feel how frozen he was. It looked like whoever had cast this sleeping spell on his kingdom had certainly done a good job at it. He had the power to ignore the spell, so at long last he took advantage of that.

"*Anfurizu!*" Xanthus grumbled under his breath. And then the King was finally able to move and stand up. The King had been asleep for nearly a week and up all night last night trying to gain back his ability to move. But he had had no choice but to use magic. Call him a hypocrite for killing all those druids and magic folk, but he used magic often. And it was his secret, and no one would ever know about it. Not even the love of his life, Queen Anne. But now was not the time to think of that.

Xanthus stood up quietly, sneaking out the door cautiously. He was heading for the dungeon, where he would gladly kill a few druids while he was at it. It was at long last that he'd be able to do so! Within a few days, they would all be dead and this mission would be accomplished.

CHAPTER EIGHT

He had awoken Anne and lied about how she had come to. He told her that the spell must have worn off on them and that it would probably wear off on the others eventually, and then took her to the dungeon. They entered the underground prison and Xanthus immediately spotted his greatest enemy; Avyrus, the druid King.

"Ah, Avyrus," Xanthus smirked at the druid King tauntingly. "Are you enjoying your stay at Xanthus' dungeon?" The King wondered how they had eaten for that one week of having been asleep. Perhaps the sleeping spell had taken away the hunger for them? It made sense.

Avyrus did not reply; his face was filled with hatred. It was no wonder, after all King Xanthus was responsible for all this. It made him swell with pride. He knew that he had fulfilled part of his quest to destroy the druids when he saw the leader's unhappiness.

"I see the young magic boy has stopped yapping," Xanthus laughed energetically, referring to Titus. "That is good. Let my methods teach him well!" The King then looked Avyrus dead in the eye. "I should exalt him for it."

"Speak poorly of us all you want, it will not change anything," King Avyrus turned his head away from the evil King with disgust in his facial expression.

Looking in at the druid's cold, icy blue eyes made him smile with satisfaction. "I do not want it to change you," Xanthus stated, and then added, "No, I am already happy knowing that you and the rest of the druids will never leave my castle fortress!"

"We will find a way," the druid King growled confidently. He was so stubborn! Couldn't he just accept that he would never again see his lovely forest, which by the way was not so lovely anymore because of the fire? That this would be the last place he saw before he was executed?

"Xanthus! Hurry over here immediately!" Queen Anne called to her husband with a serious voice. It startled him, especially the tone. Leaving his arch enemy to do whatever it was that imprisoned druids did at that time of day, he went to meet his pregnant wife at the front of a prison cell. "What is wrong?" He asked worriedly.

"The cell is empty!" Anne said quickly, and Xanthus looked into the prison cell. He was shocked to see what he saw; the King was completely sure that this was the jail cell that Titus had been residing in. He recognized the servant that lay asleep where Titus should be. It was his wife's servant, Millie. And what lay next to her was a big dish of half eaten food. It looked like it was the King's missing dinner of rice and two chicken legs! How dare Millie share it with a druid, no less a prisoner? This was bad. It meant that Titus had escaped, most likely given a key by Millie.

"And look!" Anne distracted him from his thoughts facing a cell behind him. "Another druid is missing also!"

"I've had enough of this," Xanthus snapped, fed up with the disappearances. He stormed back to Avyrus' cell. "What do you know about Titus and the other druid escaping? Tell me!"

"I know nothing," Avyrus said simply.

"You must know something! You had to have been awake with the yapping of that damn druid Titus!" The King persisted angrily.

"It may come as a surprise to you but I was asleep when Titus escaped prison."

Xanthus took out his sword, its silver edges flashing, and hit it against the bars where Avyrus stood. Luckily on the druid's part it did not hurt him, but the King of Aerulis wished it had. He could do with the druid bleeding a bit for all he'd done. "I will not accept that!" The King snapped furiously.

"Sire, please!" Anne cried to him, obviously disturbed by her husband's sudden violence. But he ignored her, waiting for what Avyrus might do or say next.

"I swear, I was asleep," Avyrus replied, but then added, "But I know that wherever he is... Titus and the other druid will find a way to free us all from you."

"Those worthless boys can never defeat me alone," Xanthus chuckled.

"No, but perhaps... well, perhaps a certain wolf can," Avyrus spoke quietly. A wolf...? What was getting into Avyrus' head? How could a wolf defeat him? It was hilarious to the Aerulis King. Titus and the other druid stood a better chance of winning than a stupid wolf!

"Okay, Avyrus, you can go dream about how your wolf will rescue you from your cell," Xanthus mocked his enemy and then turned away to walk upstairs. "The execution will be held in a few days. Your druid warriors could be anywhere by now, so I won't bother with a patrol to fetch them."

"What about Millie?" Anne queried.

"Leave her!" He growled sternly. "She's a traitor. And traitors don't deserve to be moved from a cell." His face softened, and then he walked back down the stairs and put his arm around her. "Come now, forget about all this nonsense. You need rest if we want to have a healthy child." He led her carefully upstairs and then made their way to her chambers where he laid her down to rest. They kissed goodbye and then he left the room to go off and set up the execution. Once he was out the door, he whispered something that would clear off the spell completely so that he may continue with the day. It would take quite a while to set up the execution, maybe even until midnight that night, but it was worth any wait.

They were so lost! They'd walked so far, yet had come across absolutely nothing useful. Titus never liked not knowing where he was, and since he was leading Zachery into unknown potentially dangerous land, you could certainly say that he wasn't in the greatest mood he'd ever been in. For the past week they'd probably been traveling in circles, hopelessly lost in the forests of England. They hadn't even come across a single kingdom! It was either Aerulis was as big as the entire human galaxy or that every kingdom had magically disappeared. None of those stories were possible, so what was going on?

"Titus, just face it! We are lost! Can't you just ask someone for directions?" Zachery pressured him. He'd been saying that the entire trip! Titus would have stopped and asked for directions if there was someone to ask.

"Oh, okay," Titus mocked him with frustration, "How about we ask the speck?" The druid warrior growled, pointing to the dust speck floating around in the light. "There's no one here!"

"Then let's find someone!" Zachery snapped back at him.

"Haven't we been doing that for the past week?" Titus threw his arms up impatiently. "No, how about *you* go and find someone. I'll keep going."

"We can't split up," the young druid warrior Zachery responded sternly. "King Avyrus would be disappointed. We are out here to save the druids, not act like immature apprentices."

"Spare me of your lectures, Zachery. You and I are barely warriors ourselves," Titus retorted bitterly. He understood that Zachery had lost his father to Xanthus' men very recently, but that was no excuse!

"The wolf that I raised is out there somewhere," Zachery began, gesturing to the forests and mountains ahead. "I know of the prophecy, my father told me. If we find her, she will help us. I know it..."

Titus raised his brow. What? Avyrus and Tairek had brainwashed him too? What had happened to his intelligent druid friends? So this is what the druid clan had come to. Stuck in a rotting dungeon, awaiting execution, thinking a wolf would rescue them. "You believe that also, Zachery?" He sighed.

"Trust me, Titus," Zachery told him. "Sascha will save the druids, somehow."

"So where are we going now?" Titus asked him, treating Zachery like he was the leader.

"I don't know," Zachery replied, and then looked forward at a mountain in the distance. "Forward I guess."

Titus glanced at where Zachery was looking. His heart sank when he saw the snow covered mountain tops. "Oh no, you can't be serious!" He exclaimed with disappointment.

"And why not? Wolves usually hang around the mountains," Zachery grinned with amusement. He walked forward, continuing their quest. Titus just stood behind, mouth open with shock. But he snapped out of it and followed.

"So we're going over the ice cold mountains," he growled. "Someone put me out of my misery, please."

They'd been walking for hours! When would they reach the mountain? At least at this point it wasn't that much further, then they could take a rest... maybe even rest for the night as it was nearing the evening time. It was twilight... and Titus didn't want to sound crazy, but had the trees suddenly become black and leafless?

From where Titus was in the strange forest, he could finally see a lit up city and a huge castle in back of it. "Windstorm City," Titus recognized it. He had been brought there as a child to meet King Dragomir who was the only ally of the druids. He had been about seven years old then, now he was nearly twenty. "I wonder how King Dragomir has been doing all this time."

"Maybe he'd be able to help us?" Zachery suggested.

That was a good plan! That's what they'd do instead of searching for a hopeless wolf! "Yes, I agree," he told Zachery, and then took off running toward the city entrance. Finally, they had something to work on. Dragomir would send his army of knights to rescue the druids from King Xanthus, and now Titus didn't have to worry about a thing.

They walked through the city as if they were native to Windstorm. When they finally reached the castle they were greeted by about five guards. "Peasants are not allowed to access the castle grounds," one of the strong guards clad in metal armor growled sternly. "I suggest you turn around immediately." The guards held up their swords as if to ward off the "peasants".

"You don't understand," Zachery told the Windstorm City guards. "We're here to speak with King Dragomir. We are druids."

"You are druids?" The tallest of the guards seemed shocked. "I have received word that they were taken captive by King Xanthus de Taske. Then how could you be a druid?"

"We both escaped," Titus told the guard.

"And we have to find a way to rescue the rest of us!" Zachery added. "So please, let us speak with your King."

Some of the guards exchanged glances with each other. Titus knew that they were debating whether it was safe to let the two druids in. Of course, they had no intention of hurting anyone.

Soon, the tallest guard turned back to them. "Very well, follow us," he growled with a low suspicious voice. "But do not try anything stupid. We will kill you immediately." And so, Titus and Zachery went on to speak with the King about their situation.

CHAPTER NINE

"Retreat, Twilight Pack!" The mysterious deep voice screeched over the wasteland. There was blood everywhere. It was a horrible battle so far, many wolves had died and not many dragons had been killed. It was almost a lost cause, a worthless effort. But Sascha would not let it get to her head. She needed to win... she needed to find Akemi.

The bloody white she-wolf looked back toward the mountains, seeing a brown male wolf with pale underfur. "Thor!" She yelled to him. A few dragons flew overhead and breathed fire over the battlefield. They were setting everything on fire! It looked like the dragons had the upper hand now. The hot flames surrounded her, burning at her pelt but at the same time hardly touching her. What could she do now? There was no way to escape! It was too hot! The dragons screeched as they trapped the other wolves in the flames, and she didn't know if any of them were to die there or not... but if she were to help them, Sascha needed to find a way out of the cramped flame circle she was trapped in. She glanced around, desperately searching for an opening in the flames. But there was nothing there. No openings, no exits. "Jump through the fire Sascha!" She heard Thor on the other side of the fire.

"Are you crazy?" Sascha exclaimed with disbelief. Jump into the fire? How was she actually expected to do that? She coughed; the smoke was getting to her. She saw memories of the fire in Rosewood Forest the night the druids were detained by King Xanthus, that horrible night. Tairek said that he'd always be there with her, but where was he now? He was not here! Not even in spirit. She didn't feel his presence. She just felt the heat of the flames that threatened her life. The flames that she needed to jump through. She didn't have the thick pelt of a wolf for she was only half wolf; her father had been a dog... and so that made her less protected against the fire.

Sascha dashed forward, aiming at a thin wall of flames. She could see a figure on the other side of it but she did not know what it was. It was a silhouette, but it was large and it was shaped like nothing she'd ever seen before. It had long ears, or something that really resembled ears or horns. The first thing that came to her mind was a dragon, but it looked different from the others. But whatever it was, if it was anything at all, she would brace for it on the other side. Shutting her eyes tightly, she took a real leap of faith through the bright red flames. It barely burned her for she was passing through them so fast. Only a little black smoke was left emanating from her as she hit the ground on the other side, and her red and white fur was stained black with soot in some patches.

Sascha almost forgot about everything else as she saw the silhouette moving. It raised itself, head going up higher and higher. It literally stood at the height of a cedar tree! "Are you ready to fight me, you pathetic parasite?" The thundering voice questioned her fiercely.

It truly chilled her to the bone. But she only knew one answer. "I was born ready, Harloc," she snarled loudly so that the powerful Ituic Dragon could hear her well.

"Very well," the evil creature growled. "Then let me squash you!" Sascha saw a huge hand full of extremely long claws coming down directly at her, and she immediately rolled out of the way, being careful not to touch the flames with any part of her body. She felt the intense tremors in the earth as Harloc's hand impacted the ground. She looked up just in time to see a large jaw of razor sharp teeth the size of bananas coming down at her, and leaped to her paws and raced away in less than three heartbeats. Harloc's face smashed through some of the earth, getting a pile of rotten dirt and pebbles stuck in his mouth. Roaring louder than thunder, the sinister dragon creature spat it out quickly. The white she-wolf had caught a glimpse of his face and replaying the image in her mind again and again just scared her out of her fur. His vibrant red eyes, hairy face, orange-and-blue mane, and his huge horns that protruded from the back of his head. Even in the evening darkness she could make out almost every mannerism of Harloc, thus fighting just as well in the darkness as in the light. Of course there was the light of the flames, but that didn't help her see the dragon's upper body.

"Are you just going to dodge every attack I throw at you?" Harloc snapped.

Sascha snarled, her long fangs showing. The essence of battle was burning within her. She felt a great need to win the battle with the evil dragon. If she made it out of this wasteland alive she would head straight back to Aerulis and kill Xanthus, the one who had caused her life misery since the beginning. It would be over. She could return to her life with the druids as normal, only then she would be a much wiser wolf than before. She'd be able to protect her clan with everything she had, instead of cowering in the corner like a mouse.

Unfortunately she could only jump as high as the creature's chest. Though the power in her legs was very strong, she still had trouble jumping up to the height of Harloc's throat. If she could do that, then everything would be finished just like that. So how was she expected to kill Harloc? Make him bleed to death with her fangs that barely did anything to even the smaller dragons? If only the rest of the pack could help her...

"Sascha! The rest of us are fine! Don't worry!" Thor yowled to her through the flames. She looked behind her to see through the blurring red flames and saw that every wolf and dog had been accounted for. Of course she knew that a lot of the canines had died in the fire, never mind the entire battle, but that was the way of war. Wolves died, and there was nothing anyone could do about it sometimes. She owed it to Thor for building up courage and coming to help out. If he hadn't, many more warriors would have died.

"Look out!"

It startled her and quickly she whipped around. But it was far too late. Before she knew it, Harloc had her in his deathly jaws. That was a bad move of Sascha! She should have been paying attention! Curse her inexperience! Curse it! As if she weren't in enough pain already, Harloc's sharp sword-like teeth ripped through her flesh down to the bone. She was so high in the air! It was as if she were on the highest branch of a majestic sequoia tree, thinking that balance was the most important thing in the world. But at this point, she would have been more than happy to fall... the pain was so intense, and she was losing a lot of blood from this.

The long pointy teeth were jammed into her shoulder area and her hip area, and luckily her extremities were not hurt in the process. It was a miracle! Harloc threw her plummeting to the ground from that height, the white she-wolf crashing to the ground agonizingly. Within seconds there was a pool of blood around her almost lifeless body. Visions of the past were flashing before her eyes; her friends, the druids, Tairek's untimely death... she knew it was the end. It was over. All of this struggle... it had been for nothing. She had known it was pointless from the beginning, to even think that saving the druids was even possible.

Don't give up now!

The strange sound rang in her head, sending chills down her spine. There was a familiarity in the powerful voice; Tairek! She now recognized his gentle voice. Shifting her position a little bit, she tried desperately to stand but couldn't. "Tairek, I can't... I just... can't go on doing this anymore..." The pain was just too intense, and she knew that eventually she would die. She was ready for death though, it was not one of her fears anymore.

Just trust me! The druids are alive and well! They're waiting for you to save them!

"But how can I save them? I can't even kill a dragon!" She protested quietly.

Don't think like that! Think of the prophecy, Sascha! Get up! Get up and fight!

Sascha felt a new inspiration forming within her. Tairek was really here with her, just like he'd promised before he had died by the river shore back in Aerulis territory. She could not let him down... Sascha would never forgive herself if she did. He had died so that she could begin the quest to save the druids.

You didn't have much time to train with Rei before the dragon attacked, but everything you need to know has been in you since your birth. I didn't realize that when I gave you the bag of coins. Don't worry; just let your instincts guide you!

A new strength pulsed through her. She had to live! And she had to win this battle! Everyone needed her. The druids had to be saved from their execution. Zachery her beloved caretaker had to be rescued. And the druid King Avyrus. She clawed and thrashed on the ground, struggling with all the will she had to stand up. Ever so shakily, she eventually stood up straight with her mange ridden bloody tail pointed upward.

"Are you ready for more?" Harloc snickered, his huge teeth bared pompously.

"Always," she snarled furiously and then charged forward, digging her claws into the earth to increase her speed. Drowning her mind with thoughts of the druids and all the happy memories before everything had gone wrong, she sprang as high as the power in her hind legs would allow her, and fortunately that height was very acceptable. A dragon's chest area was a very good place to attack, she had learned. She sunk her long fangs deep into the Ituic's chest. She remembered what Tairek had said, he had said that the important fighting moves had been in her since birth... and so she let all worry fade. She decided to try something new.

Harloc roared with anger, but she didn't care. Not when she had come so far and was closer to winning than ever before. Digging her sharp back claws into the dragon's skin she started to rapidly climb up its neck, every few seconds grabbing the skin with her teeth for support in case she slipped. Of course Harloc's wounds were starting to bleed badly, and that was a good thing for it proved he was not immortal after all. She climbed up so quickly that Harloc didn't even have time to decide what to do. She reached his throat almost immediately, and did only what she could. She sank her fangs into his throat, tugging and ripping strongly. If she could stop the dragon's breathing then it would be finished.

Harloc was caught by surprise, but the shock only lasted a split second before he fell over and tried to pull her from the wound with his hand. Sascha couldn't hold on, his grasp was too strong for her. She felt as if her body would rip apart if she continued to hold on to the Ituic's throat. She just hoped she had broken the airway. Harloc coughed in a fit of pain which made him weak for a moment, so the white she-wolf took advantage of that and scrambled out of his grasp. Sascha raced for the gigantic opponent's head as it lifted up, and leaped up to bite down on Harloc's ear. Sascha was getting very hot while in the battle circle that was surrounded by the fire, so she was thankful for a sudden breeze that cooled her a bit. She saw Harloc's face, and still thought it was rather creepy. His eyes were glowing red with cat-like pupil slits, and his face was dusty with reddish orange scaly skin. His mane was orange with blue highlights, and was blowing slightly in the light breeze that picked up.

As Harloc began to stand Sascha leaped over the dragon's head and sank her fangs into what she could of his large muzzle. Harloc shook her, quickly panicking. He sped through the flames holding his head very low to the ground so that Sascha would be burned and perhaps forced to let go. Dragons were apparently immune to fire because Harloc was not harmed. Fear pulsed wildly through her, and she acted completely on her instincts. Leaping away from Harloc, she was especially careful not to breathe in the flames. She landed on solid cold ground less a second later, her once beautiful white fur completely black with mucky soot. Somehow her fur had been protected, and she presumed that Tairek had shielded her from the dangerous fire as she passed through it.

A dragon roared in the distance. They were returning? Sascha was having a hard enough time fighting one. She had an eerie feeling in the pit of her stomach... maybe this really was the end?

CHAPTER TEN

"You are both great warriors, traveling through the wilds for seven days to save your Clan," the King of Windstorm city said in reply to Titus and Zachery once they had finished their story. "My deepest condolences go to Zachery. Tairek will never be forgotten by any of us." The Fighting Master Rei stood by the King, trying to hide his grief. Apparently he was going to grieve for Tairek the great druid physician. Titus remembered him from his last visit to Windstorm City when he was just a child. Rei had barely been in his early twenties then.

"Sire, we are very in need of your knights. If you could join our fight to live, you would be in our debt forever," Titus dipped his head respectfully. It was different when he was staring nobility in the face then when he was just relaxed in his clan. When he was relaxed he was a smug, pompous jerk even if he didn't want to admit it... but when he was here, in Windstorm City, he felt as if he played the part of his mentor King Avyrus of the Druid Clan.

Dragomir seemed to think for a moment, contemplating whether he should send out his knights to Aerulis to fight a cause not his own. But Titus knew that King Dragomir and King Avyrus had always been allies in the past, and it would be a betrayal if he failed to send out his men to rescue them from the murderous King Xanthus.

"Very well," the King agreed finally. "I will send my knights. However, if the battle becomes unbeatable for us, we will retreat. Understood?"

"Yes, your majesty," Titus answered, nodding.

"Good," Dragomir said and then gestured for his knights to go, "You will leave for battle immediately."

"Yes, sire!"

The dragon flew closer to her, nearly touching the ground with its huge legs and tail and wings. Dust was kicked up from the wind caused from the rapidly approaching dragon's wings, or at least where the dust could be kicked up for most of the land was in flame now.

This was it... she couldn't handle another dragon. Harloc was almost more than she could handle. It had been a good shot, with Tairek's inspiration and her own determination to save the druids; and so, she prepared to let go...

But the dragon roared over her, heading for Harloc instead. "What?" She whispered to herself with confusion. What was the dragon doing? Wasn't it going to kill her? Instead it was heading for its leader. She turned to see what the dragon was doing exactly and was surprised to see it slamming into Harloc and knocking him to the ground. Sascha saw that Harloc's throat did not appear to have been damaged.

Harloc quickly dislodged his warrior's pinning grip and kicked him almost all the way across the fiery field. Now that had to hurt! The poor dragon had probably broken a wing or two... after all, he was trying to help her and the pack, or at least she thought he was.

"Kuro, you bloody traitor!" Harloc was already up and flying toward Kuro the dragon that had tried to help her, not a scratch on him aside from the wounds that Sascha had inflicted. "All traitors will die!"

Not while I'm here, she thought furiously. The white she-wolf raced after the dragon and leaped upward over the flames. Just as she had sunk her fangs into Harloc's leg another dragon came out of nowhere and pushed its leader to the ground, this time with its long teeth dug in tightly.

Now all those dragons that had seemed to disappear had come back. One dragon, a blue dragon with purple eyes, lent Sascha help; it picked her up and flew over the field of flames. It blew white breath out its mouth hastily, and she was surprised to find that it turned the blazing hot fire to freezing blue ice.

Sascha saw the opportunity and leaped out of the dragon's hands and down onto the frozen white fire, sliding almost unstoppably on the ice. She struggled to regain her balance and at the same time tried to dodge all the wavy formations of former fire jutting out. The ground rumbled wildly as the broken dragon struggled to break free from the ice that froze him to the ground, and with a shatter he flew up into the red sky. Ice shards were sent everywhere and pierced the ice like a sword slashing skin. Sascha leaped out of the way of every one of them, swift as a fox.

"Harloc, I'm down here!" The white wolf snapped up to Harloc who flew in the sky looking at all the dragons headed his way. They were turning against him! Now the pack had the power of over fifty dragons against Harloc!

The sinister Ituic turned, his face radiating with the most heated rage she had ever seen on someone. He was about to charge down at her, to collide with her into the solid ice.

"Harloc...!" Kuro's enraged voice rang out before the big creature could attack Sascha and he immediately smashed into his leader, falling out of the sky. Kuro was okay! There was not a scratch on him! As she ran to the site where they would crash to the ground, she saw Kuro get a hold of Harloc's shoulder. He ripped out a chunk of shoulder flesh, blood pulsing out of the gigantic dragon's wound. Sascha was very pleased with this. She would not have expected Harloc's entire horde to turn against him so quickly and willingly like that, but it was very nice of them. She would have to thank the survivors for what they'd done after the battle was over.

Sliding quickly out of the way the two dragons crashed to the ground, frost and sharp ice shards being sent up in the air as they impacted. Kuro flew instantly out of the ice cloud, leaving his half dead leader covered in icicles and blood. Harloc moaned in pain, struggling to stand.

"You shouldn't have tried to kill my pack!" An angry voice roared over the ice.

Sascha looked beyond Harloc's massive body just in time to see Thor leaping up a few feet attempting to sink his teeth into the horrible creature. To Sascha's terror, Harloc immediately lifted his huge hand and slashed the Twilight Pack alpha away powerfully. But... wait! A long spatter of blood shot up from Thor's neck as he crashed to the ground twenty feet away from the dragon. Sascha raced passed Harloc to come to a halt at the alpha's side.

"Don't bother, you pathetic white blob!" Harloc snarled painfully, blood pooling below him from his severe shoulder wound.

Sascha didn't reply and just checked Thor for his wounds. "Are you okay?" She asked frantically. He didn't reply and that intensified her concern for him. Thor's upper body was already covered in scarlet red blood. When Sascha found his wound her eyes widened. His... throat was...

"Thor!"

"It's about time I killed one of your warriors!" Harloc snapped. "My own warriors are as weak and stupid as you are!"

"Shut up!" Sascha whipped around, white fur bristling with hatred. She stared straight into the Ituic's red eyes, not noticing how the dragons of Doragontaigun were surrounding the two from a distance. "It ends now, Harloc! You've built up all your god-like power, but it counts for nothing now!"

Harloc seemed to brace himself for Sascha's attack, standing up straight and balanced, awaiting the white she-wolf's move. The Ituic's giant teeth were bared, and Sascha had to admit that they definitely intimidated her a bit. But she didn't care. Thor was dead because of this monster! She charged forward, digging her claws into the ice for better balancing, and when she was in striking distance she jumped up. It must have been the determination, or maybe the anger that pulsed through her right now, but all she knew was that she was going higher than she had ever seemed to go. Outstretching her right paw Sascha unsheathed her claws to their full extent, hearing

Harloc's roar as he extended his head toward her as she flew toward his upper neck. When they impacted together, Sascha drove her claws deep into his neck, eventually reaching his windpipe.

Just like that, it was over. Less than two or three seconds' worth of recent combat and Harloc was about to die. At long last, the surrounding kingdoms of this barren wasteland were at peace. Thor's death had been avenged.

Sascha ran up toward Harloc's massive head, where it lay almost lifeless on the numbingly cold ice. She looked into the Ituic's blood red eyes, the depth of them being so deep it was like staring straight into a crystal clear ocean all the way down to the bottom, thousands of feet down. It sent chills down her spine, and she felt unease well in her chest. Did Harloc really have that power in his eyes alone? To make others feel fear when facing him eye to eye? "I am not finished… beware of my return," the dragon's old ear piercing voice choked out.

"What do you mean?" Sascha asked with concern, just before the light in his red eyes died away. Was he trying to say that he'd haunt her? Or that he'd seek revenge on her in other ways? Right now, it didn't matter... she couldn't believe it... she had won the battle!

"Thor! Thor, wake up!" She heard a very familiar voice and turned around to see the gray speckled she-wolf and the rest of the huge platoon gathering around their dead alpha's body.

"Akemi," she ran over to her, leaving Harloc's body on the frozen plains of ice. Akemi did not look up at first, still looking at Thor. She never liked seeing her friends suffer, as the Twilight Pack leader's death was a great loss for the gray she-wolf. Sascha pressed her muzzle into Akemi's shoulder, as if to reassure her it was going to be alright.

"I'm glad to see you, Sascha," Akemi said quietly, filled with grief and happiness at the same time. She sat down and curled her fluffy gray speckled tail over her big paws. "Thank you for doing all this to save me... all of you!" She added and turned her head around to address the entire platoon. Only then did Sascha realize with horror at how low the numbers had dropped; there seemed to only be around fifty total warriors in the pack now! There had been nearly two hundred before the battle! So many lives had been lost to kill just one dragon.

"Wait a second," Chino came up behind Akemi, followed by a slim black and brown dog with pointy ears. "Who is the leader of the Twilight Pack now?"

"Yes... who will take over?" Akemi asked the huge mastiff. "I never got to see who became next in line."

Then, a familiar face emerged from the crowd of wounded warriors. "I am," said the solemn white faced male wolf. "I am Talomi, new alpha of the Twilight Pack."

Akemi's eyes brightened with pride and affection, coming over to bow before the ice blue striped male. "Talomi is the new alpha of the Twilight Pack! Does anyone have any objections?" The gray speckled she-wolf yowled to the platoon. Everyone howled their approval of their new alpha. Sascha was surprised that their howls hadn't reached back to Aerulis.

"Talomi! Talomi! Talomi!" she called into the cheerful air of victory and happiness, letting the wolf in her take over as she howled to the moon above her.

It had been a few minutes before the howling died down. Talomi came up to face Sascha. "I must thank you for saving my pack," he said gratefully. "We all wish you luck on your journey to save your druid clan."

"Always, Talomi," she told him. "If you ever need my help again, you can find me in Aerulis, perhaps in Rosewood Forest."

Akemi approached the white she-wolf happily. "My loyalty will always be to the Twilight Pack. Thank you all for trusting me enough to rescue me from Harloc. However, I must make a complicated request to my leader," she said and turned to Talomi with wonder in her aqua blue eyes. "I would like for your permission to take a battle patrol to Aerulis. You know of Sascha's prophecy, right?"

Talomi flattened his ears with uncertainty. "We've just barely won this battle," he said softly. "Are you sure we'd be able to handle another battle?"

"I don't know," Akemi responded, lowering her head. "But the prophecy is very important to Sascha, and even to us in a way. We don't know what Xanthus could end up achieving in his lifetime if he remains King. After all, he is still young."

"So you think Xanthus will try and conquer more than Aerulis' territory?"

"Yes, he might... and the fact that he hates druids and wolves scares me..." Akemi said. "He might try and kill us if he gets a hold of Windstorm City."

Talomi sighed, very reluctant to let a patrol travel to Aerulis to fight. "Very well," he said, dipping his head. "You have my blessing."

"Thank you, leader," Akemi responded, dipping her head respectfully.

Suddenly all of the dragons came into view and settled down from their flight beside the huge pack. "Wolves not have to fear," one of the dragons said, lowering its big head down to see the wolves better. They apparently didn't entirely know the wolf language, but enough where Sascha could understand. "We bring wolves to battle."

With the moonlight shining on Sascha's glistening white pelt, she couldn't help but let out a smile. There was no way they could lose now with dragons on their side.

CHAPTER ELEVEN

Akemi's fur was fluffed up in the harsh wind as the dragons soared through the cloudy night sky. The dragons had allowed the wolf patrol to ride them all the way to Sascha's kingdom of Aerulis, which was over one hundred miles away. But when riding a dragon, the possibly two day journey would turn into a short flight. The dragon that was carrying her on its back was ice blue with white highlights and purple eyes. She was very beautiful, slim and sleek in the air. She had told Akemi that her name was Sky Wing, which was just perfect for her colors and air speed.

Sky Wing dropped down a bit, going under the dragon formation. Akemi lost her balance and dug her claws into the ice dragon's skin but not breaking the skin, blinded by the increasing dark and misty clouds that blew weightlessly into her face. She screamed with fear, lowering her belly fur down on Sky Wing's back. "Don't do that!" She begged.

"Wolf no fear," Sky Wing reassured her confidently.

If anyone here was afraid of such great heights it was Akemi, but she forced herself to relax and kept a good grip on the female dragon. In fact, she wrapped her paws around Sky Wing's skinny neck. The ice dragon rose up again, flying in line with the huge formation. She saw Sascha ahead of her, riding on the jet-black male dragon Kuro. Sascha had explained to her that somehow he hadn't been injured by Harloc when he had first turned on him. The heroic white she-wolf was just a short distance between her and Sky Wing. Akemi was proud to call her a friend. Sascha had risked her life to save her from Harloc, who had used her to lure the Twilight Pack and Sascha into his territory. Itachi had been the one to take her captive and bring her to what the dragons called the Meadows of Agrona just over the mountain. Now that Harloc was dead the Meadows would grow back to its lush and beautiful form. Perhaps even become a little forest of birch trees or even twilight firs. It was very hard to get to but perhaps if the Twilight Pack was driven out of their territory they could move over the mountain and into the Meadow where the dragons lived. Obviously there was an alliance between them now.

Sky Wing caught up with Kuro and Sascha. They kept a good distance between themselves so that their wings did not collide together, flying side by side through the skies over Windstorm City. "What is Aerulis like?" Akemi asked Sascha.

"It's very beautiful," Sascha answered. "I lived in the Rosewood Forest." Rosewood Forest sounded like a nice place for a wolf pack to live. That might also be a possibility for the Twilight Pack, to come live there if they ever needed somewhere to go and the dragons weren't around to help them. The gray she-wolf imagined the trees of pine and maybe oak, and a hollow log with roses growing from it, thus earning the forest's name Rosewood.

Suddenly, Sascha seemed to see something down below. Akemi followed Sascha's gaze down to the ground and saw a long line of knights were leaving the city of Windstorm behind. Was it because of the dragons flying above them? Akemi felt fear rush through her chest and the fur along her spine stood up.

"Wait a minute," Sascha sounded bewildered. "I think I know the two men following close behind!"

"Huh?" Akemi raised a brow with astonishment. "The knights here are killers! Don't play around with them!"

"The ones I know aren't knights!" Sascha replied with the biggest smile of happiness. "They're druids."

There were druids in Windstorm City? Following a huge band of knights? That sounded strange. There had never been a druid in Windstorm, at least not in over a decade. "Huh?" Akemi repeated more quietly.

"Go down to the ground and follow the knights," Sascha told Kuro, and within an instant he flew quickly downward.

"Sky Wing, can you follow Sascha?" She asked quickly, and the ice blue dragon did as she was asked. Akemi yelped with fear as Sky Wing dropped out of the sky and started to fly over the moonlit green land of the kingdom of Windstorm, but she held her awkward grip on Sky Wing's slim neck.

Sky Wing landed gently on the ground beside Kuro, the wind from her wings causing the nearby trees to sway back and forth. Sascha leaped off Kuro, approaching the knights that had stopped in front of them. Akemi jumped off also, happy to have her paws touch solid cold earth again.

Akemi's heart sank when the men screamed and yelled, pointing their crossbows at the two dragons. Kuro snarled and Sky Wing lowered her head, backing away slowly. No human could understand the words of animals, as far as Akemi knew. Except maybe Fighting Master Rei, the man that had trained Sascha before the gray she-wolf had been taken captive by Harloc's horde. But he wasn't around to translate a bark, so they were in a bit of trouble. Kuro and Sky Wing could easily kill the men, but they knew not to go against Sascha's wishes... unless it became vital that they turned and flew away.

"Please! Don't shoot!" Sascha begged, and then winced in pain as she tripped on her bad arm. It was her left arm, which had apparently been caught in Harloc's mouth when he'd picked her up in his deathly jaws. But unfortunately, as it had been for every wolf since the Creation of the Earth, the humans could not understand her and so her words were nothing but a pitiful bark to them.

"Sascha, we need to get out of here," she growled to her white furred friend sternly. "You must be mistaken about your druid friends being here."

"No," she said quietly, and then her green eyes caught something in the crowd of knights. "Titus, and... Zachery!" She added with the greatest euphoria, dashing toward her friends. Some of the knights shot at her, but even though she was wounded Sascha was able to dodge and jump out of the way of every one of them. Akemi was filled with worry; especially when one of the arrows nicked the top of Sascha's slim back. What she was doing seemed impossible! How did she possibly dodge human arrows? It was almost unearthly. But there had to be an explanation; perhaps the druids were known to be very sleek and skillful in those parts of Aerulis and Sascha had picked up on it?

When she finally reached the two men she had spotted, she unintentionally spooked the horses a bit and barked playfully toward them. Akemi couldn't tell which one was Titus and which one was Zachery, but for druids they were both fine looking humans. They didn't look as ratty and mangy as she had pictured forest men to look like.

"Don't shoot the wolves, sir!" A dark brown haired man with green eyes said loudly to the captain of the knight platoon.

The knight captain looked bewildered. "It is a wolf, why shouldn't my men kill it? It looks like a wolf-dog, and all wolf-dogs must be killed."

"I raised this wolf. Her name is Sascha, and she is as much of a druid as I am!" Zachery shot back at the captain, getting off his black horse and kneeling down in front of Sascha. He patted her over the head, scratching behind her ears, ignoring the fact that his hands were becoming scarlet from the remaining blood on Sascha's white fur. Akemi had forgotten that her white furred friend had washed herself in a puddle of melted ice to get the dark colored blood and soot off her usually glistening white pelt. However, the stinging wounds still remained. And they would take a couple of days to fully heal, perhaps even a few weeks.

Zachery pulled Sascha gently into an embrace, not wanting to upset her open wounds. "It's been so long..." Sascha said quietly, her voice barely audible to Akemi. "I've missed you so much."

Akemi slowly approached, extremely nervous to be greeting a human in a friendly way for the first time in her life. Her head was low, ready to flee if the humans tried anything. "You've met a friend, have you

Sascha?" Zachery smiled, his face being covered in licks and kisses by the white she-wolf. He slowly moved his head toward Akemi, crouching down and not moving a muscle. To him Akemi was a strange wolf who had not been socialized with humans, and that was true... but of course she had no intentions of harming the two men.

"Come here, girl," Zachery said calmly to the gray speckled she-wolf, slowly reaching out his hand for her to catch his scent. Akemi flattened her ears uncertainly, glanced worriedly at Sascha, and then looked back to Zachery. She outstretched her head, sniffing his fingers and then pressing her cold nose into his hand.

"What are you, a wolf whisperer?" Titus asked sarcastically. "Wolves hate me."

"Maybe you're just not patient enough with them."

Titus rolled his eyes. "Okay, perhaps you and King Avyrus were right," he said with embarrassment. "The druids will be saved by a white wolf."

"At last you've figured that out!" Zachery laughed, patting Akemi on her gray cheeks. It was a very dangerous place to stroke a wolf, for at any moment the wolf could turn on him and bite his extremity; his wrist veins. But of course Akemi would never do such a thing to anyone unless she had to, and alas she had no reason right now.

"Yes," Titus growled quietly, and then went on with a mocking voice, "and I see they've brought dragons with them."

Zachery didn't seem to be bothered by the dragons, and Akemi did not know why. Humans didn't usually like dragons and for obvious reasons. "Perhaps that is all part of the prophecy," he said in response to Titus' comment.

The knights seemed to become bewildered by his words. Titus narrowed his eyes. "You've lost it!" The druid warrior snapped.

Titus' horse reared on its back legs as suddenly Kuro and Sky Wing advanced toward them. Akemi ran back toward them, waving her tail. "Can you tell them our plan?" The gray speckled she-wolf inquired hopefully. "We don't need the knights of Windstorm City to fulfill what we were born to do ourselves."

Kuro nodded his head and looked over toward the knights and Titus and Zachery. "Wolf says that knights not needed," he spoke in the tongue of the humans. These dragons were very knowledgeable. "Dragon horde will accompany wolves to battle."

"I do not understand how a wolf could speak to a dragon and convince it to fight for it!" Titus said to Zachery.

"Whatever the reason, we should listen," Zachery replied and stood up. "Avyrus, and Tairek, would be disappointed if we didn't."

"So you are willing to give up Dragomir's army and rely on a wolf pack instead?"

"It sounds crazy but it isn't!" Zachery retorted, turning around to face the amber eyed druid. "My father would not have received word of the prophecy if it were not true! Deal with it!"

The sound of many wings came into earshot and all of a sudden the wind nearly threw some of the knights off the horses. "There are more dragons!" The captain yelled with horror, riding up to Titus and Zachery. "I am sorry but my men cannot help you! We have not even left our city yet and we come across dragons. It is a bad omen!"

"They not hurt you," Sky Wing attempted to reassure the knight captain, but it was too late. He was already gone along with the rest of the knights, retreating back into the city of Windstorm.

"Well, now that you've scared away our only way of winning the battle against Xanthus, we may as well give up," Titus said to Zachery. Didn't he just say that he believed Sascha would save the druids? Akemi let out a very quiet frustrated growl.

"First of all, how many times do I have to tell you?" Zachery sighed with annoyance and grabbed his horse's reins and patted its nose to comfort it. "Second, didn't you promise a certain woman that you would return for her?"

"N-none of your business...!" Titus stammered in reply.

"The white wolf defeat Harloc the evil Ituic Dragon," Kuro explained, ignoring the bickering of the druids. "That reason for wounds. Then we go Aerulis to defeat King."

"Sounds good to me, I guess," Zachery commented. "How are we going to get there? I've had my fair share of walking..."

"Maybe we'll become dragon riders!" Titus sneered.

Sascha ran up to stand by Akemi and looked up at Kuro. "Let the druids know that they have the plan right. If it is okay with you, Kuro and Sky Wing, then I would like you to carry Titus and Zachery all the way to Aerulis," the white wolf-dog barked, flicking her tail excitedly. She added with a chuckle, "So... it looks like they won't exactly be dragon riders."

And so Kuro told the two druids what they were going to do. Titus and Zachery were not too thrilled about being carried by a dragon one hundred and twenty miles through the skies at a very high speed toward Aerulis. The dragons would be going at the speed of eighty miles per hour, and humans did not handle that speed well, especially with the hard stinging wind in their face. But was there any other choice? Akemi knew that Sascha couldn't just leave them here, they were practically her family.

The gray she-wolf wondered if she would do the same for her own family members, like Strawberry her sister for example... and she decided that she would have done it. Her parents may be dead, but she would never have left her siblings behind. Zachery and Titus, the two druids, were of great value to Sascha.

And so, they set off once more. Titus and Zachery were carried by Kuro and Sky Wing all the way to Aerulis. The rest of the dragons followed, the hunger for the great battle seeming to show in their eyes as they flew toward their goal.

CHAPTER TWELVE

In the next few hours a harsh blizzard blew in, as the season of winter was coming upon England quickly this year. The white moon was heading down toward the dark indigo horizon, beginning to set on that fateful night. It had witnessed a great battle and would return the next night to shine upon the wolves' victory over Aerulis.

The wolves made it within the borders of the kingdom of Aerulis, soaring through the blizzard. Akemi could be seen holding awkwardly onto Sky Wing's neck, as if she would fall at any given moment. Her gray and dark gray speckled fur was frozen with snow and ice and her ice were closed to the smallest slits to protect her fragile aqua blue eyes from the stinging wind and white crystallized snowflakes that blew in her face. To keep herself busy in the white nothingness up in the air she thought of likeable things, like how no snowflake would ever be the same as another and how a snowy valley looked when the weather was clear and sunny. It was the wolves' favorite weather, especially for hunting. Up in the blizzard she could not hear Titus' whines of fear anymore, which was a relief to her. He was starting to get on her nerves.

Sascha was still riding the black dragon Kuro, the first to turn against Harloc and attack him. He had somehow managed to not get wounded by the huge sinister Ituic and that was a great benefit to both the dragon and the snow-white wolf dog. Wolf-dog... ever since the captain knight of Aerulis had mentioned it Sascha had started to think about her heritage more and more along the way in the lonely blizzard sky. She knew that she was part dog, of which breed she was uncertain, but Zachery had once said that she looked like a cross between a wolf and a white German shepherd dog. And unfortunately she had taken on the anatomy of the German shepherd.

"We should land!" Sascha yelled through the blizzard clouds. "The storm is harsh and we've been flying for hours!" And so the group descended downward, landing in a forest. Despite the cold Sascha began to warm up a little when she recognized the burnt remains. The druids should have been there then but instead King Xanthus de Taske had taken them away from their rightful land. This was the place that she had called home, and would continue to call home once this was all over.

Akemi approached the white she-wolf. "So what are we going to do now?" She asked, speaking over the high wind and snow that blew recklessly through the air. "The patrol is very tired and wounded, just as you are."

Sascha knew that they could not go into battle in these conditions, especially with untreated wounds and more to come in the following battle. "We should rest here until twilight tonight," she answered, turning her head to glare into her friend's aqua blue eyes. "Maybe by then this blizzard will pass through, and we will be rested up."

"Is everyone feeling okay?" Sascha asked her gray speckled friend who sat just outside the remains of Tairek's old Medicine Shed, dashing across the snowy druid clearing. After the wolves and dragons had trudged through the snow in search of the druid camp, Sascha had asked Akemi to look after the wounded wolves in the patrol. Ever since the fire that had destroyed the forest the druid camp had been completely burnt down, and that angered her very much.

"Strawberry's wounds are hurting her badly," Akemi answered, standing up from her sitting position beside the burnt shed and glaring worriedly into Sascha's deep green eyes. "Everyone in the patrol is complaining of sudden stinging in their cuts, bites and scrapes. Riza has the worst wounds, and I have been worried about her from the beginning. She should never have come due to them."

That was not a good thing. Sascha knew that they would have to find warmth somewhere in the camp before frostbite set in, and at the same time they had to worry about horrible wounds and infections. However, it was a good thing that the wolves and dragons had rested up a bit since trudging through the snow trying to find the camp. "We will need herbs for them," she said, blinking away the slow falling snowflakes. That was another good thing; the blizzard had cleared up since they'd first arrived. "The only one here that knows about herbs I think is Zachery, and we need to ask him." Before Akemi could respond to her words Sascha added, "Go fetch Sky Wing."

Then Sascha sped off through the clearing in search of Zachery while Akemi went off to find Sky Wing. She found him at the edge of the clearing on top of the King's Rock where Avyrus used to make his announcement. A fallen burnt leafless tree was all that was left of the majestic great oak tree that jutted out of the ground beside the large rock. It was splayed across the rock face, broken and full of black soot even with the snow on top of the bark. Xanthus had done this... all of it, and he would pay for what he'd done.

Sascha barked to get his attention and saw the physician apprentice lift his head to acknowledge her. He looked troubled, and she assumed that he was just mourning his father now that he was home. She could definitely say the same, being back in the druid camp brought back many good memories. She would continue to mourn Tairek's death for years to come, perhaps even for the rest of her life. Sky Wing and Akemi arrived just behind Sascha a few moments later and the white she-wolf said to the blue dragon, "Tell Zachery that we need his help with herbs." And Sky Wing did as she was told.

"What herbs wolf need?" The dragon inquired after telling the human what they needed.

"We need something to prevent infection," Akemi answered.

"Wolves need prevent infection," Sky Wing added to Zachery.

Sascha waited patiently for her friend to answer. She knew he knew the right herb by heart, but after all this chaos it must have been hard to transition from a warrior to a physician in a matter of seconds. "I believe Tairek told me that the right herb to prevent infection is the Calendula Flower," he finally said. "It is rare and only grows near Silver Lake at the other end of Rosewood Forest, unfortunately a long travel from here. Shouldn't take you more than a few hours to fetch it and come back," he paused, probably trying to remember its appearance so that the wolves would recognize it much easier. "It is a very beautiful flower. Its petals are bright orange and long like that of a sunflower. It is almost... fluffy. You'll know when you find it!"

"Thank you," Sky Wing dipped her head appreciatively. "I go find flower and bring back." She spread out her wings and flew up swiftly into the sky.

Sascha was grateful for the dragon's help, and also amazed at how quickly Sky Wing returned with the orange Calendula Flower. It had only taken her about forty minutes to find it and return back to the druid camp. Sky Wing handed Sascha the precious flower and Akemi showed Sascha to where Riza was lying on the ground in the shelter of the Medicine Shed. There was not much space in here now that it was half caved in from the fire but at least it was generally warm and safe from frostbite. Only the wolves that needed the most attention were resting in the Medicine Shed; Strawberry being one of the five wolves in there aside from Riza. The wounded she-wolf was ginger with lighter underfur, and she reminded Sascha of Thor. Was it possible that Riza could be Thor's daughter? She also had blue eyes like the former pack leader which sparkled like the brightest night. It was obvious where the wound was; a long bloodied streak ran across her right side.

With the Calendula Flower held between her teeth lightly, Sascha sat down beside Riza and placed the flower down beside her. "Do we chew and apply it as a poultice or does she have to eat it?" Sascha asked her gray friend.

"In the Twilight Pack we usually apply herbs as poultices to wounds," Akemi replied confidently.

Sascha sniffed at Riza's gaping wound. It would have to be cleaned before she applied the poultice. What was the point of applying an herb to bloody fur? "Does it hurt you?" She asked.

"Yes, very much," was all Riza could choke out.

"I wish I could give you poppy seeds after this, but it's snowed too hard by now to find poppies and the supply Tairek had has burned up," Sascha flattened her ears apologetically.

"I'm sure I'll manage," Riza said quietly, wincing in pain as the wound throbbed on her side. As gently as she possibly could the green eyed white she-wolf placed her long pink tongue on Riza's still bleeding wound and started to lick slowly. After a few seconds the ginger she-wolf started whining, but then stopped. Sascha assumed that she had remembered to try and maintain her pride for she was a warrior of the Twilight Pack.

"Do I chew the stem or the flower?" Sascha asked after she had fully cleaned Riza's pelt.

"I'll bring Zachery in," Akemi said and returned with the physician apprentice a few minutes later.

"What do you need me to do?" He queried, crouching down on his knees to be on the same eye level of the wolves.

Sascha pressed her nose to the Calendula Flower and then moved the tip of her black nose just above Riza's wound, as if trying to tell him that they needed to apply the flower as a poultice.

"Ah," Zachery observed and then picked up the flower in his left hand, careful not to harm it. "You take the stem and crush it, and then add it as a poultice on the wound. Then you take the flower and have the patient eat it." Still holding the flower, the physician apprentice went around the big shed and found a wooden cup that Tairek used to crunch herbs for their juices in.

Sascha took the flower from Zachery and once the cup was placed under her mouth she immediately started to chew the green stem. The taste was foul on her tongue but she knew she had to do it… so she bore it for the sake of Riza. They needed all the healthy warriors they could get right now. It was a patrol of twenty two, and she didn't want it to decrease to twenty one just yet. When every inch of the Calendula stem was chewed up, nothing was left but the flower's juices in the wooden cup. Then Zachery took it away, shaking it gently and careful not to spill a drop. "It is winter so some of the juices have dried up from the cold," he said with a neutral face. "But this amount should still be enough."

As he slowly poured the juices over Riza's wound, the ginger she-wolf quietly howled in pain. "It's okay, girl," Zachery said soothingly to the wounded wolf. "It may hurt now, but give it a few minutes... the pain will go away and you'll feel much better."

Sascha was surprised; she had never seen Zachery treat a wolf before. He did it so well, so carefully... as if Riza were human. Tairek had probably taught him to respect all animals, even the fierce and dangerous wolf. Wolves were only dangerous because most of them did not trust humans, but the wolves that had been told by Sascha would never look at humans the same way again.

"Are you sure you can trust this man?" Akemi growled into her ear with a serious tone. "What if he's actually killing Riza?"

"If you trust me, you should be able to trust Zachery," the white she-wolf replied to her gray furred friend. "He raised me, and he's a trained physician."

"A physician…?" Akemi tilted her head and raised a brow in confusion.

"It's the human equivalent of a healer," Sascha explained.

"What are you two chatting about?" Zachery chuckled, smiling at Sascha and Akemi.

"He's baring his teeth at us!" Akemi flattened her ears, lashing her tail angrily.

"Calm down. That's just the way humans smile, baring their teeth," Sascha responded. "It's strange, but he doesn't mean it in a harmful way."

Zachery detached the round orange flower from the chewed up stem and placed it beside Riza's muzzle. "Eat this," he said quietly.

Riza sighed miserably, obviously not wanting to get the herb taste all over her tongue. Wolves would never naturally eat plants so it was incredibly disgusting for them, more horrid than it was for humans.

"Come on, it will prevent the infection," Zachery encouraged her, scratching softly behind her thick ginger ears. "You want to be the best warrior you can be, right?"

"He's so good with wolves," Akemi sounded truly astonished.

"His father was good with animals also," Sascha said, smiling as she remembered Tairek once again. "He must have gotten it from him." The white she-wolf looked back to Riza and found that she was already half finished with stuffing the fluffy round flower down her throat. A tear fell down the ginger wolf's face in disgust but she kept it up until the entire thing was briefly chewed and swallowed. "That was the most horrid thing I have ever tasted in my life!" Riza barked with clear unhappiness.

Sascha smiled. "But it will still help," she said.

"I wish I had water to drink," Riza whined. "This taste will stick for hours if I don't."

Akemi stood up and flicked her tail. "I'm sorry but there's no water near here," she explained. "It's all frozen. And you can't eat the snow, because it'd give you hypothermia."

"But I'm thirsty!"

"We all are, come to think of it," Sascha commented.

"Yes," Akemi responded, and then a few moments later pointed her nose toward Zachery who crouched there comforting Riza. "You need to get him to treat the others."

When she heard Akemi say that Sascha knew that it would be a long day, and it wasn't even noon yet. They had no herbs so Sascha would probably have to go out with at least two less wounded wolves to search for a good supply, in the beginning of winter at that, and try to communicate with Zachery.

As the day progressed and it eventually became noon time, the wolves had found some of the herbs that they needed. Titus had lit a fire just outside the Medicine Shed which offered a wonderful warmth to all wolves that gathered by it, huddling and sleeping. They needed it now more than ever; for once twilight broke upon the world it was time to move out.

Jasmine, a golden colored dragoness, had brought a mouthful of Calendula Flowers and dropped them at the Medicine Shed so that Zachery could work with the rest of the wounded wolves. Sascha had gone out with Stone and Hikaru looking for moss and had luckily found some by a frozen pond growing on a large boulder, having to dig through the snow that surfaced the rock to find it. They hacked a hole in the ice just beside the boulder and soaked all the moss in the water, then headed back to camp. Sascha knew that everyone was thirsty and that they would be very glad to drink from the moss.

When the three wolves returned Sascha saw Titus beside the fire surrounded by almost the entire patrol, the winter sunlight beating down on his black hair. Staring at him as Stone and Hikaru went inside the Medicine Shed to give their moss to the most wounded wolves, Sascha kept her green gaze on the druid warrior. She had never seen him look so strong and mature. He looked as if he were Avyrus the druid King, sitting beside the wolves and staring solemnly into the noon sky. The druid clan did not have a prince as Avyrus had no sons yet, but Titus looked so much like the King, it was hard to believe he was not related to him.

Sascha pushed those thoughts to the back of her mind and padded into the Medicine Shed to deliver wet moss to Thundermist, a she-wolf with sorrel colored patches and blue eyes. She was so happy to lap at the water, and it made Sascha happy that her temporary warriors were getting healthier by the hour. At this rate they would be the strongest wolves in England!

The white she-wolf looked around the shed and saw Riza and Strawberry drinking rapidly from the moss until it was dry. The taste of the Calendula Flower was finally out of their mouths.

"Do you need anything else?" Sascha asked the brown and white she-wolf with a smile.

"No, I'm fine," she responded softly, licking her lips for any extra droplets of the cold, sweet winter water. "Thank you."

"Anytime," Sascha said joyfully, and then turned to Akemi who was lying down beside Zachery. "Akemi!" She barked and watched as her gray speckled friend raised her head to her. "Meet me outside."

Akemi nodded and left the druid physician's side, following Sascha outside into the cold air. "What is it?" She inquired curiously.

Now Sascha would finally be able to ask Akemi a long overdue question. "Will the patrol be able to fight tonight?" The white she-wolf smiled hopefully. "You don't know how grateful I am for you convincing Talomi to grant you these strong warriors. I'm proud of them for their performance in the battle against Harloc."

Akemi grinned and dipped her head. "Yes!" She exclaimed enthusiastically, waving her tail to and fro. "They are recovering faster than I've seen any wolf. By tonight I assume it will be as if they were never injured. The cuts will be visible, but their strength will be undying."

CHAPTER THIRTEEN

"Is it time to go?" the gray speckled she-wolf asked.

It was twilight. It was definitely time to leave the druid camp and move in for the battle. "Yes," she said solemnly. "Gather the patrol. We move out when the moon peaks over the horizon." Titus and Zachery decided to wait with the dragons in the clearing for their return with or without the druids.

"Okay!" Akemi barked and rushed away to sort the group. When the moon began to rise, just as it had during the last battle, the patrol was divided into six wolves a line, six in back of the front line and so on. Sascha the white wolf led the patrol, much like a captain knight would. As they stood upon a large tall hill at the very edge of Rosewood Forest overlooking the entire majestic city of Aerulis under the winter sky, their moderately long wolf fur swayed in the cool light wind like flags or trees.

They had come a long way for this. They had their chance to storm the castle and take back what was rightfully theirs. Sascha could feel Tairek's presence beside her, his hand on her shoulders. The wind carried his scent into her nose, and she breathed it in happily... she had missed his smell.

Sascha turned to face the patrol, her face beaming with anger. Her tail was erect straight up in the air, her fangs bared with immense aggression. "The King of this city has stolen what is precious to me," she snarled with rage. "At long last it is time to steal it back." For some reason, Sascha felt as if the knights of Aerulis knew that she was coming somehow. "Pack, you do not have to fight in this battle if you do not wish it!"

All eyes were pointed attentively toward her and the patrol was soaking in every word she spoke. "If it is our destiny to die," the great white wolf continued, "then so be it. But let history remember that as a wolf pack, we chose to make it so!"

The patrol cheered, barked, and shrieked their approval when she had finished. "FOR AERULIS!" The white she-wolf howled. When the cheering died down a bit, Sascha expressed her plan for the castle raid. "Riza...! Distract the guards at the drawbridge, and have Hikaru and Stone sneak up on them to knock them out!"

They dipped their heads in agreement.

"Once they're knocked out, the rest of the patrol will move in quickly through the city!" Sascha continued loudly. "Akemi, Snowdrop, and Izor; I will sneak in the back way into the dungeon where you will fight the guards off. I will knock out the dungeon master and take his keys, then set every druid free!"

"And what are we supposed to do?"

"Yeah, are we just supposed to keep fighting while you just wander the dungeons and open prison cells?"

"Yes, you are," Sascha said to her patrol. "But I promise you; once I have released the druids I will lead Akemi, Snowdrop, and Izor to the courtyard for battle. Then, I will go find Xanthus... and kill him."

And so, the patrol moved out. They ran down the hill and out of the forest, unsheathing their claws and digging them into the earth to increase their speed down the steep slope. Barking and yapping like feral dogs they soon approached the gate to the city of Aerulis. Sascha skidded to a stop and spun around to face the battle patrol. "Halt!" She barked sternly, her ears as pointed as a snowy peak. They obeyed her, stopping quickly and holding their heads up high with as much honor as she would see in the eyes of a strong, noble knight. They awaited her very first order as a battle leader patiently, some flicking their tails back and forth. Their paws were under the snow, already so cold that they felt a bit numb. A few specks of white snow clung frozen to their thick fur. "Hikaru, Stone, sneak through the city and do as I told you both," Sascha ordered solemnly. "When you've cleared out the drawbridge area, please send us a signal to move in."

"Like a howl?" Stone inquired quietly, approaching the white she-wolf with his sister Hikaru by his side.

"No, that would alarm the knights in the castle," Sascha disagreed and then thought for a moment. When she spoke again she tilted her head a bit. "Perhaps... you could actually go a little farther than the drawbridge?"

"What do you mean?" Hikaru questioned.

"On the side of the courtyard there are stairs leading up onto the ledge that overlooks the kingdom and Rosewood Forest. You should be able to see us from there," the white she-wolf explained, her green glare flashing importantly. "Guards pace those ledges all the time, so you'll have to watch out for them."

"The point being...?"

"At all four corners of the castle there is a watch tower attached. There is a guard in each one of them, looking over the land in case another kingdom attacks," she went on to say. "Knock the guard out there. I believe that there is a lever one of you can pull down that sends off a ball of fire into the sky. We will take that as our cue that everything is clear. Everything understood?"

The two siblings barked their agreement and then scrambled under the open space in the gate. They rushed off into the city, careful not to be seen by the unknowing villagers. They waited for about twenty minutes, anxiety clinging to their pelts. Sascha had faith in the two wolves, but she hoped that they wouldn't fail and be caught by the knights. Then suddenly with an ear splitting sound a large ball of orange flame shot up into the air from the watch tower on the right side of the castle. That was their cue!

"Okay!" Sascha growled to her patrol, lashing her tail with seriousness. "Listen up! Organize yourselves into a single file line. That was our cue to move into the city. We have to hurry!" As the great white wolf bounded toward the gate, the patrol gradually developed a single file line. Sascha slithered under the gate, the wolves of the battle patrol following close behind. Akemi was the first to slip under the gate, Riza behind her, then Izor, Strawberry, Tsute, Siber, Raven, Thundermist, Sorrel, Evia, Shin, Jason, Tasgall, Amara, Snowdrop, Zuri, Aeron, Yorath and Kira.

They raced through the city, unseen and unsought for. It reminded Sascha of the time she ran through Windstorm City trying to find the Master Rei while escaping the guards. Except now it was a peaceful trip because they were not being chased. Soon they reached the drawbridge and Sascha sent the patrol into the courtyard, but removed four from that group and hurried eagerly to the back of the castle. The snow almost hid the small iron barred opening but they were able to find it. Sascha tried to break out some of the bars so that a wolf could fit through the opening, but she had to pull extremely hard to even get one loose. She let go of the bar and shifted her head back to her four patrol members. "Akemi," she called to her gray speckled friend to come and help her. Sascha grabbed onto the loose bar, Akemi biting onto the same one, and they both pulled.

BANG!

The two wolves flew backward, the bar still in their jaws. Standing, they spat the black bar out and summoned the small group to do the same as they had just done with the rest of the bars. There were only five bars left now and they all tried to work very hard to get them out. Their teeth ached but they ignored it. They were not going to whine about the pain, they wanted to continue their quest without stopping for a mere second. They entered the dungeon once every bar was removed.

"Okay, listen to me!" The white she-wolf growled softly to the four other wolves with her in the dungeon hallway. There were no guards pacing this little area, thankfully. "I want you all to go to the entrance of the dungeon and pick off the guards. Snowdrop and Izor! Go your separate ways and search all throughout the dungeon for people that would pose a danger to me or Akemi and Thundermist. Understood?"

Snowdrop, the white and gray she-wolf with yellow eyes, and Izor, a jet black male wolf with blue eyes, dipped their heads and raced off in a random direction in search of the dungeon entrance where the most guards would be. The rest of the wolves followed her quickly, and that left Sascha alone with her own task in the dark and moldy prison.

The white she-wolf wandered the dungeon for a short while and then spotted the dungeon master. When she saw him she had been crossing through a hallway full of prison cells, but then she backed up immediately behind a wall when she realized that he was heading her way. She felt a surge of surprise which froze her in place for a moment, her breathing picking up. It wasn't that she was scared or that she did not have faith in her fighting abilities, she was just not used to being in danger in the unfamiliar castle of the evil King Xanthus de Taske. She knew that the dungeon master had seen her, so she prepared for him to walk around the corner. When he did she leaped into his side, his head hitting the ground. The dungeon master fell unconscious, and that made Sascha switch into a hurry. She did not know how long the man would be out of the conscious, so she quickly pulled off his belt and let the metal ring with keys attached to them slide off of it. She grabbed them and rushed off to find the druids inside the prison. She didn't want to bark in case any guards or knights were lurking around there.

She picked up that strong familiar scent and followed it. It was the scent of the druids! Something that Sascha hadn't been able to smell since the fire.

Coming around a corner, the scent growing stronger, she saw the entrance to the dungeon. She saw Akemi and Thundermist at the base of the stairs that led upward into the castle, five guards knocked unconscious by the stairs that led upward to ground level. "Is everything going okay?" She asked them.

They both nodded their heads. Akemi pointed her nose toward the first cell across from the stairs. "Look," she barked.

Sascha tilted her head and followed her friend's glare to see something long awaited by her. It was King Avyrus of the druid clan. She looked around and spotted all the other druids in the cells in the hall. Finally she had reunited with him and the rest of the group. Sascha knew that they couldn't understand her, but she started talking to the handsome King anyway. "You would not believe what I've been through, Sire," she barked. "I will get you all out, I promise." It was kind of hard to talk with the ring of keys in her mouth, but she managed.

The King was sitting in the corner, looking kind of pathetic. He seemed very depressed, and mangy. He hadn't bathed in a while so he smelled a bit dirty. His hair was screwed up and looked horrible. He hadn't even bothered to run his fingers through it to keep up a decent appearance. Avyrus scratched his head, not even bothering to look up. "Leave me alone," he growled with little to no energy.

"Avyrus?" Sascha raised a brow with confusion. She could only assume he was depressed because he had been in the moldy dungeon for so long without any of his needs tended to properly.

"What's wrong with him?" Akemi asked, approaching Sascha from behind. Sascha didn't answer; she stood up on her forelegs and tried all twenty of the keys until the very last one fit into the keyhole, and she turned it and unlocked the cell door. The white she-wolf did not let go of the key that was correct for each of the prison cells. "King Avyrus, I've come to rescue you and the others," Sascha rushed into the cell once she had opened it wide, which would ensure that it would not close on them. That would be horrible, being locked in. "Get up, okay?"

Avyrus sighed impatiently, barely even noticing that the door had been opened, and looked up. When he cast his nearly white ice blue eyes upon the white wolf that stood tall before him his face filled with great awe. Sascha realized that he was just starting to recognize her. "The Great White Wolf has come to save us!" He exclaimed with shock and was completely speechless. "How...? But how... how is that..."

Sascha covered his face in wet wolf kisses affectionately. "Just give me a moment," she barked quietly. "Akemi and Thundermist will guard the entrance while I release the druids."

CHAPTER FOURTEEN

She had released the druids and had put Izor in charge of leading them to the little formerly barred opening where the wolves had gotten in. It was just big enough for a man to fit through, if he could reach it. But that was not part of Sascha's task; no, she needed to reach the throne room while Snowdrop, Akemi, and Thundermist entered the merciless bloodbath in the courtyard. The white wolf hoped to God with a stone in the pit of her stomach that no one had died... that would kill her inside if more innocent blood was shed, especially shed by the most dishonorable men in the land.

Her pads starting to ache, she came across what she presumed to be the entrance to the throne room. The big dark solid doors were locked! That made her frustrated. How was she supposed to get in? Skidding to a halt and retracing her steps back to the large entrance, she backed up against the wall on the other side of the hallway across from the doors. Let's face it, she was not a battering ram but being such a big and strong wolf she knew that she could probably beat the door open in one try. With a short distance between her and the Throne Room Door, she dug her claws into the wooden floors and raced headfirst into the doors.

SNAP!

The long wooden board inside the Throne Room that kept the door locked snapped open like a mere stick, Sascha sliding in on her belly over the shiny floor, dazed for a moment and confused as to where she was. Oh, perhaps she should not have done that...?

When she finally came to her senses the white she-wolf lifted her head wearily and swallowed down the natural fluid in her mouth. When she breathed through her nose she picked up a scent... it was a strange smell. Sascha had never tasted it before, and the fact that it carried a dark atmosphere to it put her on edge. She was afraid to look around and face the Throne Room royal chairs where the King would normally sit, even on a lonely day... for she had a good idea about who the owner of the scent was. The entire room was about forty feet from door to the royal chairs.

"Evening visitor," a sinister voice spoke soft and mockingly behind her. She knew she had to turn around and face her enemy. When she did, she saw a tall muscular man standing on his throne. His lower stomach was sort of hanging, his belt holding it in tightly, showing that he was a little unfit... just as she would picture a King. He had long, wavy jet-black hair with deep brown eyes that seemed to stare straight into the core of her soul.

"Let me be completely honest with you, wolf," the darkly King said shiftily. "I found out about your prophecy through your pathetic King, and I only started believing him when I saw the horde of wolves attack my knights out of the blue. And so, I prepared to face you."

"I can promise you one thing, Xanthus... that you will regret ever threatening my clan," Sascha snarled, her long and sharp white fangs bared with hatred and fury. She wasn't even thinking about the fact that he would not understand her. Without hesitation she rushed at him, closing the distance between her and her enemy very rapidly; only to be greeted with a painfully sudden sensation of teeth being dug into her white scruff. She did not even have a moment to understand what was going on before she was thrown half way across the Throne Room floor. One second she was leaping at Xanthus, the next she was lying flat on her side with immense confusion as to what had just happened.

"You see, I have never told anyone this, not even my lovely wife Anne," the voice of Xanthus sounded from behind her, and as she slowly lifted her head he continued. "I am a shape shifter. This is why I have been able to keep my secret for so long. Anyone that ever did find out has never survived long enough to spread the word."

Sascha regained her balance, standing up completely straight and turning her head to face the creature half way across the Throne Room from her. He was a shape shifter? She had no idea what that word meant, but she certainly knew that it meant it posed a potential danger to her if she was not careful enough. Sascha's green eyes slightly widened with surprise, her ears rotating backward. Xanthus had transformed into a black muscular angry wolf; he had a blue O shaped marking on either side of his cheeks, closest to his nose. It wasn't quite touching the bridge of his nose. The wolf's brown eyes still seemed to pierce her soul if she stared into them too long. If the King was somehow a wolf now, didn't that mean he could understand her too?

She tried to speak but the black wolf beat her to it, "I believe that you have come to stop me from killing your clan."

"I have," Sascha snarled.

"Let me end it here!" Xanthus roared and went speeding toward her. She had just enough time to face the black wolf getting closer every second and thundered toward him, her pads hitting the floor at four separate times just as all big four legged animals did. The collision between them was incredibly painful; Xanthus leaped up a little higher than Sascha had decided to, burying his fangs into the back of her neck while her teeth broke through the skin of the King's wrist. They tussled on the floor, the black male's fangs thankfully not delivering a fatal wound to her neck. Just one quick nip was all it took, really.

Sascha dug her claws into the King's chest as she was pinned down hard by him, then she reached her head up to rip his right ear clean off. It felt as if something else had made her do that. As Sascha spat out the rounded wolf ear, Xanthus jumped away from the she-wolf shrieking with pain. Scarlet red streams of blood ran down the right side of the evil King's face. He looked completely speechless in pain. "How dare you rip off my ear?" The big black wolf snarled angrily. "I... I am a married man! My wife will be horrified!"

"If she loves you I don't think she'll mind at all, Xanthus," Sascha growled and leaped at him once again, this time catching him off guard. She held him on the ground for a moment, instantly shredding his shoulder with her sharp white fangs. But Xanthus just wasn't going to give in to the pain; he lifted his head up and opened his jaws as wide as possible, clamping down on Sascha's tender side. The white she-wolf howled and tried to pull away but found herself pinned again by the huge paws of King Xanthus de Taske. She was held down so hard that she could not move her limbs or extend her head to bite his neck. She was totally immobilized except for the typical wagging movement of her tail. "That's funny," Xanthus snickered. "No one has ever been able fight me for longer than three seconds before being killed. I'll have to give you a gift for the effort."

Suddenly the Throne Room doors burst open.

Sascha and Xanthus froze with surprise. The white wolf was pleased and horrified at the same time. Pleased because of who it was, horrified of what might happen to him if he stayed around.

"Sire!" Sascha exclaimed before Xanthus put his jet-black paw on her throat, halfway cutting off her windpipe. Fortunately she could still somewhat breathe.

It was King Avyrus! She could hardly believe that he had traveled into the castle Throne Room just for her. She knew that she was supposed to save the druids and everything, but why had he risked his own life to come back for her?

"My clan and Aerulis have been enemies since King Richard, your father, died and left you the throne," Avyrus snarled a new fury in his voice that she had never heard in anyone before. "I have lost everything! My father, my best friend, control of my clan, my peace of mind... but justice will be served." Avyrus' tense, deep icy blue eyes shifted from the black furred King to Sascha. "You, Sascha, the Great White Wolf of Britannia... you will restore the peace here, and prevent an everlasting age of darkness over all of Great Britannia and beyond."

"Enough!" The big black wolf snapped. "That was the prophecy. That is not reality."

"We will see about that!" Avyrus retorted.

Sascha knew that it was not worth trying to talk the druid King into leaving while he still had a chance of escaping alive, for she could not speak English to the man. She lacked that ability unfortunately.

Still unable to move Sascha barked up at Xanthus, his paws pressuring her throat a little less by now. "Please, don't hurt Avyrus!" She begged him.

The shape shifter King stuck his muzzle in her face. "The 'hero' is begging, eh?" Xanthus teased and then turned back to Avyrus. "Say goodbye to your wolf pet."

She quickly tried to remember Tairek's words to her while she was fighting Harloc, the great Ituic Dragon who formerly terrorized the kingdom of Windstorm. She would not let him down now, of all times, just because she was a little wounded and being pinned by the traitor King of Aerulis. She was not going to lose!

Xanthus stared sinisterly into her eyes with an evil grin before reaching down, attempting to tear out her throat.

'Get up! Get up and fight!' Tairek's words exploded into her ears. She felt that the love for her friends and family and the determination of a true warrior was all she needed to complete this battle and win. These

thoughts were entering her mind rapidly, all of them passing before the one eared King could get a grip on her throat. With all of her strength she freed her back legs and kicked Xanthus over her head, sending him flying across the floor toward a window. Luckily for him he didn't go high enough to go through the window.

Sascha took advantage of this precious moment; she got up and charged at him with a hissing wolf roar. She bit into his neck, her fangs going deeper and deeper as she kept thinking of everything he had done to her and especially the druids. But he fought back, even through the horrible agony of the fangs embedded in his neck and very possibly throat. She tried to hold him down but he was just too strong. At least she still had a good strong grip on him.

Then a paw landed a hard painful blow to her temple, knocking her down. Sascha was dazed for a moment but caught a glimpse of Xanthus running toward the Throne Room exit. Avyrus was frozen in place, as if he were preparing to meet the black furred King in combat. "Get away from him!" Sascha snapped, stood up, and shot after Xanthus. "Your battle is with me!"

The King stopped in front of Avyrus and turned around to face the wounded white she-wolf. Right before Sascha leaped to deliver a killing bite Xanthus transformed back into a human and instantly pulled out a sword and pointed it straight at the white wolf.

She should never have jumped so quickly knowing that Xanthus could change his form at any given moment. But she could not go back on what she had done now, it was too late...

The sword pierced the left side of her chest and entered out her back. Xanthus let the sword drop to the floor, hitting with a clang.

"There," Xanthus growled proudly. Then the King turned to Avyrus who had a look of horror on his face. "Looks like your next."

No, please...don't...hurt...him...

Everything faded to black.

CHAPTER FIFTEEN

There seemed to be no gravity in this place. It was warm and bright but wonderfully so. Sascha had absolutely no worries about what had just happened, but still remembered it. Where was she?

She opened her eyes to the most beautiful place she had ever seen in her life. The warmth seeped into her skin, caressing her with the greatest amount of love. Every pain in her body was completely gone and her wounds were nothing but simple scars. The blood stains from the two previous battles were gone to. The white wolf blended in perfectly with the pinkish white clouds and sky. As she stood up she began to see a stunning, tall golden gate.

Could this be Heaven? She wondered curiously. When she remembered the druids she found that she cared for them, but also never wanted to leave this place. It was too wonderful.

"Hello, Sascha," a soft voice sounded up ahead. The white she-wolf poked her head up over some passing clouds to see a barely visible figure moving toward her. She found that it was a male with brown facial hair and yellow green eyes.

"Tairek, you're here!" Sascha exclaimed joyfully and bounded after him. When she reached him she stood upright and placed her front paws on each of his shoulders, covering his face in licks. "I felt like I'd never see you again."

"You will always see me here, and every other druid that has died," Tairek answered with a smile, scratching behind her ears. That was her favorite place to be scratched, and he was her favorite person to do it. "But you can't stay here. You must go back and complete your prophecy. You are almost finished!"

I can't stay? Sascha thought with great disappointment. She didn't want to go back! Anything but that! She loved this place. She had never felt the presence of God in a place so much as here. For it was Paradise.

"No, I want to stay!" Sascha protested, climbing down from Tairek. "Besides, I'm sure the druids can handle it from here, right?"

"Yes and no," the former druid physician said calmly. "If you stay here, everyone except Avyrus will escape Xanthus' grasp. But he will strike again, and so your journey would be a waste."

"And if I go back?"

"If you go back the druids will never be bothered by him again," Tairek responded.

It was the biggest decision of her life. To leave Heaven and go back to that horrible world, or stay here where she wanted to remain for all of eternity with no pain or suffering or illnesses. Then Tairek's next words made her feel like he had read her mind:

"Your time will come someday. And when it does, we will spend all our time in Paradise until Heaven is brought down to earth after the end of the age, where we will live forever and ever. But now is not your time."

Sascha sighed unhappily. "Then I will go back."

"Never give up, Sascha, you're almost there! Your goal is right before you!" Tairek shouted to her as he faded away into the light.

She was pushed back hard by someone that she could not see, but she assumed that it was God. And as suddenly as she was out, she was back in her body.

With a huge gasp for air she lay on the floor in a pool of her own blood. The sword that the malicious King had killed her with was gone. All the wounds were back on her skin, stinging her painfully. The first emotion that she felt was anger... for she did not want to be in this place. Heaven was so amazing, and now she was back in this chaos.

There was one good thing though, something that didn't exactly surprise her that much. Her chest wound was just a scar now, despite how unrealistically quick it had turned from wound to dead tissue. So once again her fur was completely scarlet red as blood.

Suddenly hearing the sound of swords crashing together she stood up slowly. Xanthus was fighting the druid King. But she could not understand why it sounded like Avyrus had a sword also. Perhaps the shape-shifter King had handed him a sword, to make it more like a fair duel?

She spotted him by the royal chairs fighting Avyrus. The King knocked him to the ground and looked like he was about to dive the sword through his heart just as he had done with Sascha. The white she-wolf attacked him off guard by using the move Rei had taught her; leaping up at him and aiming at his center line, pinning him to the ground without sinking her fangs into his throat as Rei had described as a last resort move. Xanthus was horrified of her sudden appearance from the dead, therefore unable to fight back. Sascha raked her claws over his face, leaving four skinny streaks of blood.

"I killed you!" Xanthus gasped with pain and horror. "How did you..? What happened?"

Sascha smirked. This was her chance! "It just wasn't my time."

With that she fell onto her left side and kicked him hard with all four paws across the floor into the nearest stone wall. He fell unconscious on impact.

Avyrus came up behind her but did not touch her. She turned to face him, seeing the deepest respect flash in his eyes. She'd never seen that before, and it had definitely never been expressed toward her if she had seen it. "You've done it, wolf," he said gratefully. "I never should have begun to doubt you."

She was very glad for his praise. "Thank you," he added with a smile.

Even though she did not kill Xanthus, she had still fulfilled her prophecy. Now the former King would be put in the dungeons and locked up until his fate was decided. By who, she had no idea. Without a King Aerulis would be sent into chaos, especially with the news that a wolf defeated their sovereign.

And so, Avyrus and Sascha headed to the courtyard where everyone was still fighting. The moon shone above the warriors, casting its chilling light upon all of the land. The white wolf was horrified when she saw all the blood on the ground. She saw that only twelve wolves remained. The rest of the wolves lay dead on the ground, fatal sword wounds to almost every part of their body. Everyone immediately stopped fighting and turned their attention to Sascha and Avyrus standing at the castle entrance.

"Knights of Aerulis," the druid King started loudly so that everyone may hear him. "Your King has been defeated! Your sovereign is down!"

"The King is dead?" A shriek of fear erupted from the courtyard.

Sascha looked for Akemi in the group of knights and wolves. She finally spotted her in back of some humans. "Akemi!" she called to her gray speckled friend. Akemi came up to her from the crowd.

"Did everything go well?" Her friend asked.

Avyrus interrupted their conversation as he spoke to the knights. "He is not dead. He is unconscious. He will be moved to the dungeon."

"I take it that it did," Akemi chuckled. "Do you need me to help?"

"Yes," Sascha answered. "I want you and a few other wolves to move Xanthus down to the dungeon. Lock him in the cell closest to the entrance, the one Avyrus was in."

"Yes, Sascha," she said and then summoned two other surviving wolves, hurrying into the castle.

Then the most dreadfully familiar voice sounded from the crowd. An approaching knight made his way through the group to the bottom of the steps that led up the door entrance of the castle. His name was slipping her mind. But she had a bone to pick with him.

"You think it's so easy to defeat the Aerulis bloodline? Even if it was that easy, Queen Anne would take over, and then her son, and then his son and so on! King Xanthus is still the sovereign. He has protected us from those evil magic folk!"

"Sir William," Sascha hissed. He had killed Tairek!

Tension filled the air as she wondered if Avyrus would reveal Xanthus' deepest secret. She hoped he would, it would benefit their situation somewhat. "I have something to tell all of you," Avyrus began slowly. Sascha had a feeling that he was going to tell everyone of Xanthus' traitorous secret. "Your King is not all that you think he is. He prosecutes the druids, and yet he himself is a magic user." Cries and shrieks of outrage erupted from the knights.

"You're lying!"

"How dare you accuse our King of such a crime?"

"Liar!"

"Traitor!

"Horrible druids!"

"I am not lying to you!" Avyrus shouted over all the protests angrily. "I have seen it for myself. He was fighting against Sascha, my wolf here, as a wolf himself, a shape shifter. If you don't believe me that is *your* problem."

"I will not take the word of a druid," Sir William broke in. "Nor will I believe that the King was fighting against a wolf. That's what *we* are here for!"

Avyrus growled. "Now, I have another thing to announce." Sascha wondered what it could possibly be. What he said next surprised her and yet made her extremely proud and happy at the same time.

"A long time ago my father and my mother met and they fell in love. Some of the older knights may remember it. My father was the great King Aeolus of the druids, and my mother was the Irish Princess Keeva," Avyrus explained with an unreadable expression. It was a cross between happiness and sadness. "For those who do remember her, you were lied to about her fate. She was never killed. In fact, she lived to give birth to me. Although Keeva died of a strange illness when I was only a boy…"

"I remember her!" An older looking knight spoke up from the crowd. "Are you trying to tell me that the knights that went searching for her were lying? How dare you accuse them of that?"

"Because it's true," Avyrus growled defensively. Sascha just stood there with a smile on her face. She could tell that Avyrus felt much better with that off his chest. But she knew that he must have had a big point behind it that no one really understood. "What I am trying to say is that I am of two royalties."

She understood what he meant now, but what exactly were his intentions?

The doors behind her burst open and she turned to see Riza, one of the surviving wolves that had gone with Akemi to bring Xanthus down to the dungeon. "He's locked in a prison cell now," she reported. "Ready for whatever you wish upon him."

"Good," Sascha smiled. "...Thank you."

CHAPTER SIXTEEN

The nine casualties that day were Tsute, Thundermist, Sorrel, Shin, Aeron, Kira, Yorath, Raven, and Zuri. The druids returned to their own camp for the night, Titus and Zachery waiting for them. The dragons were still there, sitting there in the clearing patiently. The rest of the druids were startled, but Zachery calmed them down and told them that the creatures were their allies.

Back in Aerulis the druid King Avyrus stayed in the chambers of the traitor King, Xanthus. Sascha and the remaining wolves guarded him as he slept that night so that no one may harm him. Everyone took turns guarding the King's chambers while the others slept when it was not their turn. Sascha was extremely glad for the long needed rest. She was so drained she couldn't even shift to move position when she was sleeping.

However, when she was awake and on guard millions of thoughts passed through her mind. What had Avyrus tried to get across earlier that night? And why was he sleeping in the former chambers of Xanthus? The only thing that she could think of was that he was planning to become King of Aerulis due to his royalty, which certainly was not a problem with Sascha. Anyone but Xanthus de Taske! Plus Avyrus seemed to have more experience.

The next morning, just before noon, Sascha was just waking up when she heard the chamber door unlock. She lifted her white head; ears pricked, she watched who walked out of the bedroom. Avyrus appeared and almost immediately turned his glare to the great white she-wolf. "Morning," he whispered quietly to her, careful not to wake the other wolves. Akemi was on guard at the moment but she didn't pay any attention to Avyrus or Sascha. "Follow me; I want to talk to you."

And so she did. He led her into the outside halls, a beautiful cold winter breeze finding its way into the walkway. There was snow all over the foothills in the direction opposite of Rosewood Forest, and the trees in the forest where she had been born were covered in blankets upon blankets of heavy snow. There had been a heavy blizzard the day before.

Up ahead there was a bench made of what smelled like maple tree bark. Avyrus went to sit on it, the expression of nervousness on his face. Sascha rotated her ears when she saw it, and she wondered if something else had gone wrong. Padding slowly up to him, her tail wagging lightly, she put her head on his lap. The druid King stroked her from her forehead all the way to her shoulders. It felt amazing, but it also felt a little strange now that she thought about how gruesomely she had fought the day before. One moment she was a bloody warrior, the next acting as a domestic pet for a man? Which was she?

But his following words made her realize that she was neither of those. "I am very grateful for you, Sascha," he said with a soft smile on his face. "Thank you. You are not a half-breed, nor are you a monstrous evil wolf. You are Sascha... the Great White Wolf." It was as if he had read her mind, her thoughts of wondering what she was.

"Tairek never lied or made a mistake when it came to a prophecy, that is why I believed him for so long," Avyrus continued with his soft morning voice. "Who knew that one day a wolf would defeat a man of great power?"

A few moments had gone by when the peaceful silence was broken by the deep sigh of Avyrus. "I've been thinking of something, and I want you to be the first to know," he said carefully. "Do you remember yesterday night when I spoke of my parentage? Keeva and Aeolus were both royalty, but of two different types. However, I wish to take Xanthus' place as the King of Aerulis... seeing as the kingdom needs a new ruler."

So she had guessed right. He did want to become King. And of course, she was his greatest supporter in that. "I think you should do it," Sascha barked excitedly.

"The kingdom will be sent into a great tension when they hear that they already have a new King. They won't be sure of you at first but once they see how great of a leader you are they will not think twice about trusting your judgment." He could not understand her, but all the same he knew she approved of his idea. She started to lick his face and all behind his ears and he started to scratch her cheeks with affection.

"I can see you agree," he chuckled jokingly. Her heart was filled with warmth as she felt things were slowly going back to normal. "I will announce it to the kingdom from The Balcony that overlooks the courtyard, preferably as soon as the druids are there. I'll have to fetch them with you as my guard."

That sounded great. Her more recent wounds were starting to heal quickly, so they didn't sting as much anymore. The area that the sword penetrated through her heart was completely and miraculously healed and nothing else remained but a scar and a long line of missing white fur. Maybe the current court physician could take a look at them, maybe treat her with some herbs to benefit her health.

And so Avyrus and the white wolf headed around the main city of Aerulis and then into Rosewood Forest, following the same path that Sascha had walked upon so many times as a pup in Zachery's care. They would be coming upon the camp soon, everything they passed looking so beautiful. She had a quick flashback of when she was only a month old seeing all the snowflakes cover the ground while everyone else was asleep. It was just so beautiful to her. Back then she would never have guessed that in exactly one year from then she would be the greatest animal warrior in the country.

Soon they reached the camp. Avyrus was surprised by the sight of all the dragons, but Sascha calmed him down by licking the palm of his hand excitedly. The first person to spot them was Zachery the new druid physician, and he went off to warn Titus of the King's presence. Titus rushed out of the King's Shed and went up to Avyrus. "It is good to see you again," Titus smiled brightly. The King had returned. Titus assumed that he would resume his title as the leader of the druid clan, but he was very wrong.

"Hello, Titus," the icy blue eyed King greeted in return. Taking a deep breath Avyrus spoke again several heartbeats later. "Look... there is something that I must tell you." Here it came. She did not know how Titus would take it, that the only King he had ever known was going to step down and leave someone else in charge of the forest.

"Come, follow me," he said quickly.

They headed away from the camp and into the forest. Climbing over mounds of snow and bushes

Avyrus and Titus followed by the white she-wolf finally stopped when the voices of the druids had faded into the distance.

"What is it?" Titus asked with concern.

Avyrus was hesitating, starting to sweat. How could telling the young druid warrior that he was not going to return as the King be so hard?

Just say it! Sascha thought to herself.

"I have to tell you something that I know I should have told you a long time ago..." Avyrus started quietly, and then gulped silently. Was that fear she smelled? "See... a long time ago I knew your mother. We were the greatest friends."

"What are you talking about, Sire?" Titus growled. "What about my mother?"

"You never knew her, she died when you were just a few weeks old," the former druid King went on. "What I am trying to say is that... Titus," that was the strongest moment of tension Sascha had ever experienced in a long time. "I am your father."

WHAT?! She widened her eyes with shock.

Titus just stared at his former King with shock. What would he do now that he knew who his father was? What would he say? How would he feel about the fact that his father was still alive? She was very anxious to find out and worried at the same time. "No," he began quietly, and then shouted. "No!" With great rage he went on with a loud voice, "My father died before I was born! I never knew him! I never knew a thing about him, not even his name! Nor did I know anything about my mother!"

"Titus—" Avyrus tried to comfort him by putting his large hand on his shoulder but the young druid warrior shoved him away immediately.

"No! You are lying!" Titus snapped furiously. All the respect that the druid warrior had once had for the King had vanished into thin air and all Sascha could see now was sadness and rage in his amber eyes. "Don't touch me! I don't want anything to do with you, ever!"

Avyrus hung his head, the words obviously hurting him deeply. Titus was his son so to hear him say these things was very painful.

Titus turned away, head facing the direction of the camp. Sascha could have sworn she had spotted a single tear drop down his face. "Just stay away from me. You are no father of mine." The druid had just started walking away when Avyrus tried to call him back.

"Titus, wait! Please!" He begged.

"What do you want from me?" Titus responded with a very cold voice.

"I am not going to be here for the clan anymore. I am not going to be their King any longer," Avyrus explained a little shakily. It made him sound weak, but he obviously was not afraid to sound that way in front of his own son. "I need someone to take over. And since you are of my direct bloodline, I need you to become King!"

"What a letdown," Titus growled. "Why can't Zachery become King instead of me?"

"Because he is not my son, and he has only been trained in the ways of a physician," he replied quietly. "I need you to lead the clan. I need you to lead them to the castle of Aerulis where I will explain everything."

Titus shook his head. "I'm sorry. If you want to abandon us, that's fine. But if you want me to take over for you, you've asked the wrong person." And then he walked away back toward camp. Sascha flattened her ears and went to press her wet wolf nose against Avyrus' hand.

CHAPTER SEVENTEEN

The rest of that day hadn't gone that well. Avyrus and Sascha headed back to the castle the way they'd come, they're limbs starting to ache from going the great distance. Discouragement seemed to be filling Avyrus by the moment and Sascha just wished she could do something about it. But she could do nothing, except watch and wait.

When they reached the castle they walked through the courtyard into the castle. The dead wolves had been removed, but had yet to be buried. The fact that the three knights that had been killed had already had a burial angered Sascha. The wolf pack had done more good than the shiny men ever had! Sascha had to see that the remaining twelve wolves helped her bury the untimely casualties.

Sascha walked up the hall to Avyrus' soon to be chambers where the patrol was still sleeping. No one was on guard anymore, Avyrus having left. "Come," she spoke softly to Akemi and the rest of the patrol. "We must bury the dead." And so they all made their way out of the castle to find the fallen wolves that were right outside the walls.

"Thundermist," Akemi whined with welling sorrow when she saw the she-wolf's body among the other casualties.

Thundermist is... dead? Sascha flattened her ears with shock. It was not long ago that the white she-wolf had given the sorrel-and-white colored wolf a patch of moss to drink from. And now she was dead?

Sascha pressed her muzzle into Akemi's shoulder fur in attempt to comfort her. The scar patch that she had noticed when they'd first met had reopened during the battle, but it was healing again. Of course it wouldn't heal properly; the scar would always be there. "I'm sorry," she whispered with sympathy.

And so they buried the wolves at the edge of Rosewood Forest, one by one. Some of them were Twilight Pack warriors; some were nomads that Sascha had gathered to fight against Harloc. It was very sad, for she knew that the wolves that had died would be grieved for in the Twilight Pack. And the others that had died would never be able to become real Twilight Pack members. They would always be considered Pack wolves at heart, and they would always be honored for their bravery.

When every wolf was buried Sascha started to speak a eulogy about the nine wolves that had lost their lives in battle. She felt horrible that they had died and that they would never be returning home. And it was completely her fault.

After the burial and eulogy was over everyone left the edge of the forest and started back to the castle. When the thirteen wolves made it there, Avyrus was above on the balcony that overlooked the courtyard. The knights, noblemen and women were gathered below to hear him. They looked a little more accepting of him... but Sascha couldn't understand why. She separated from the other wolves and made her way through the crowd to the front.

Xanthus. He was chained by his hands and feet, crouched down like an animal, on top of a wood platform directly below The Balcony. She knew that the platform was used for executions and whatever other punishments that the Kings of the past and present had ordered.

"You see?" Avyrus shouted over the yard so that all may hear him. "He admitted that he practices magic. Is that enough for you?"

She'd missed that much? To hear Xanthus say that was a miracle. It benefited Avyrus' reputation also, for it proved he was not lying about their former King.

"I don't believe you!" A woman from the crowd screeched and ran up to Xanthus. She had ginger red colored hair and green eyes, quite beautiful to be honest. When she reached the traitor King the woman wrapped her hands around Xanthus' muscular left arm. "Please! Please... tell me you are lying! Tell me you do not practice what they accuse you of!"

"I am sorry! It is true!" Xanthus exclaimed angrily. "And they can do whatever they want with me."

"And do not think I will let you go easily, Xanthus," Avyrus snapped. "I will not kill you, but I will order you to be flogged. I sentence you to exile. Travel beyond Hadrian's Wall and never return to Aerulis or England again."

"Don't hurt my husband any further!" The woman pleaded, obviously sticking by his side even after being lied to by him.

"Woman, be thankful that I am not going to execute him as I probably should," Avyrus responded sternly. "Keep in mind that I am Aerulis' new King. I am King Avyrus, son of King Aeolus and Queen Keeva."

"I am his wife! If he is to be punished, I want to be punished with him!" The former queen started to cry lightly. "You are no King of mine! I will never follow you!"

It wouldn't be the first time today that someone had rejected Avyrus. Titus had found out that his father was the former druid King and had refused to speak with him afterward. Seeing Avyrus' face it looked like it had really hurt him. Sascha couldn't imagine the feeling of her son or daughter never wanting to speak to her again. She hoped that Titus would come around.

"Very well; you will not be flogged, but you will be banished. I cannot have traitors among the court. There has been enough of that," the new King of Aerulis answered. "Guards, restrain her until further notice."

And the guards obeyed, taking the young woman inside the castle to the dungeon. She screamed and protested but it did no good.

"Wait," a voice at the entrance to the courtyard interrupted them. "A friend of mine would like to say something before you flog the traitor King."

"Titus?" Sascha whispered and turned around to see the young man with a proud smile on his face. "Geez, talk about mood changes." He sure looked happier now. She spotted the rest of the druids behind him, as if being led by him. Perhaps he had finally agreed to become King after all?

Zachery emerged from the group of druids, made his way through the gathered nobles, and approached the chained down Xanthus. "It is a pleasure to meet you face to face," he said bitterly.

"Druid!" the former King snapped. "If my men were not traitors I would have them shoot you right now!"

"They are not traitors. At least not anymore," Zachery growled furiously. "*You* are the traitor! You killed my father! And you will get what you deserve."

"Is that all?" Xanthus said unfeelingly.

"No, it isn't," Zachery scathed, then lifted his fist and punched the traitor King hard on the side of the face.

"There you go, Zachery!" Sascha praised her friend's nerve.

Later that day Xanthus was flogged, and then was banished along with his pregnant wife Anne de Taske. They were both escorted twenty miles north to Hadrian's Wall where right by the sea shore there would be one of the three gates that were spread across England. However, it took them two days to get to the Wall. But when they crossed through the gate, the thirty gate guards stepping aside to let them through, everyone was filled with triumph.

"Who are those two young people?" One of the guards asked.

"They are just two people who broke the code of their kingdom," one of the escorts responded.

They all watched for a moment as Xanthus and Anne vanished into the foot hills, all alone and stripped of any armor or weaponry... never to be seen again.

CHAPTER EIGHTEEN

It took the escorts three days to return to the kingdom. Back in Aerulis things were calming down. After Avyrus had announced himself the new King, had Xanthus flogged and banished along with his wife, the crowds were going back to their daily errands. Sascha wished that she could bring the potential threat of Sir William to King Avyrus' mind, but she was an animal. She unfortunately could not do such a thing. William did not like the druids, so someone should keep an eye on him.

Titus and the druids slept at the castle for a few days, until the knights that had escorted Xanthus and Anne to Hadrian's Wall arrived back. At about noon that day, Sascha eavesdropped on Titus' conversation with a girl she'd never met before. She was dressed similarly to the druids, but was just different.

"Hi," Titus spoke softly.

"Titus," the young lady smiled brightly.

"I've missed you so much!"

"Same here. I've missed you too!"

"I wanted to thank you for what you did for me, feeding me and helping me escape from the dungeon," he said. "What happened after I left?"

Millie hesitated, looking a little sad. "I fell asleep all of a sudden, and then the next thing I knew I was awake and locked in a cell."

"Oh Millie, I'm so sorry!" Titus apologized. "I will never let that happen again!"

Sascha could tell that he held great affection for this nice young lady. So he had gained something out of Xanthus' evil doings. He had found love. Millie put her hand gently on his shoulder, a great affection showing in her blue eyes. "There is no need to apologize, Titus."

"How can I make it up to you?" The druid King seemed to ignore her, wanting desperately to make her feel better about being locked in a prison.

A few moments passed where Sascha thought that Millie wouldn't answer however thrilled her smile seemed. "Well... there *is* one way you can make it up to me," she said with a loving voice.

Titus seemed confused at first, but eventually he gave the expression of realization. He gave a huge smile, softly taking her hand and walking out of the courtyard with her.

So Titus had a love now. Aerulis was at peace, and the druids were at peace. The Twilight Pack and

Windstorm City were at peace now. They had a few casualties, but they were still at peace.

"Hurry, Sascha!" Akemi's voice sounded behind her. The white she-wolf saw that the other twelve wolves were following her lead. "The dragons are outside the castle walls, I think they want to go back home!"

"They do?" Sascha questioned. She followed the wolves outside to where the fifty dragons stood almost towering over the castle. They were definitely gigantic creatures, but also great friends of hers. Without them, none of this peace would have been achieved... even if at first they had threatened to end all peace in England.

"We wish to return to Meadows of Agrona," Jasmine the golden colored dragoness announced.

"Oh..." Sascha flattened her ears with sadness. The Meadows of Agrona was over one hundred and twenty miles away on the eastern side of the country. She would probably never see them again. Then the white she-wolf remembered something horrible; Akemi and the Twilight Pack lived in the same area, so far away. Sascha couldn't bear never seeing her friend again!

"I know what you are thinking Sascha," Akemi frowned with sorrow. "But I must return to the Twilight Pack!"

"We take you," Kuro offered with a smile.

"Thank you, Kuro," the speckled gray she-wolf barked and then turned back to Sascha. "We both have two totally different destinies... and I am glad that I could have been part of yours." Akemi perked her ears up enthusiastically. "But trust me; this will not be the last time that we see each other. Our paths will cross again someday."

"And I look forward to that day," Sascha chuckled lightly.

And so the twelve wolves mounted the dragons and then took to the skies. As the great white wolf watched them fade into the distance until they were no longer visible she tried to keep it in mind that she would see them again. It would be a long time before she did, but she would nonetheless.

Later in the afternoon Sascha was sitting on a cliff by the waterfall. The waterfall that she had fell off with Tairek that fateful night. His body was not there on the shore below, obviously having been moved and buried by either the knights of Aerulis or the druids. Hopefully by the druids... after all, who would want to be buried by those mangy knights? How she missed him. She had died and seen him four days before, but she still missed him.

"Sascha," the cold breeze whispered.

Her ears perked up startled but she ignored the voice, assuming that it was just her imagination.

"Sascha...!" The voice was louder this time.

"What? What?" She spun around with fear, yelping when she thought she would accidentally slip off the edge into the river below. When she saw who it was her face lit up with euphoria.

"I cannot stay long, but I have come to give you the greatest power an animal can have aside from being able to defend itself," he said. It was Tairek! She did not approach him, afraid that if she did he would disappear. "I grant you the power of speaking to the humans."

"That will be extremely helpful!" Sascha smiled happily.

"Come here," Tairek said. And she did as he told her. The old druid physician put both of his hands on her shoulders and Sascha felt a shudder go through her. When it was over she looked Tairek curiously in the eyes.

"The next time you talk to a human they will understand you," he said quietly. "Now I must go."

"Please, don't go," Sascha begged softly, her tail wagging.

"When you get the chance, tell Avyrus that I approve of his choice to become the King of Aerulis, and that I think Titus will turn out to be a great King for the druids," Tairek spoke, and then his image faded away. Maybe this wouldn't be the last time she saw Tairek, or heard from him, but for now all communication with him was gone.

"Oh," the familiar voice of Titus spoke behind her by the edge of the cliff. When she turned around to face him she could see that he had just finished digging a small pit about half a foot deep. He dropped a key with the crest of Xanthus' family in the pit and then covered it, packing in the dirt. "Hello Sascha. How are you feeling?"

Sascha smiled. Now that she could speak to the humans she would take advantage of this moment. "I'm doing well now that the druids are safe," she said with a great smile, advancing toward the new druid King.

She had completed her destiny.

However, only part of it. The white she-wolf still had yet to have a family of her own, maybe start a pack or travel the world. Though her future may not have been as chaotic as her past, her journey was far from over.

O.H

December 18th, 2011

Treasure Coast, FL.

Edited For 2016 Edition – 7/4/2016

Printed in Poland
by Amazon Fulfillment
Poland Sp. z o.o., Wrocław